Cover illustration by Mike Knot mikeknot.tattoo @mikeknot

Interior design & maps by Louise Holland

Edited by Kate Vandelay

Socials @louisehollandauthor | @lahollandauthor

ISBN 978-0-6458896-4-2 (paperback)

ISBN 978-0-6458896-5-9 (electronic)

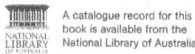

A catalogue record for this book is available from the National Library of Australia

THE DOOR

PRAISE FOR LOUISE HOLLAND

"I genuinely got this magical and almost nostalgic feeling that I can only describe as 'coming home'... Holland gently eases you into this world, entrancing you with her magical prose and expertly trickling in just the right bits of organic world building at exactly the right times to continuously spark wonder."
ESMAY ROSALYNE, *BeforeWeGo* BLOG

"...the themes within Spark of the Divine intertwine together and pay off beautifully. This novel had something to *say*, and meant it."
LUCAS LEX DEJONG, AUTHOR OF *Deluge*

"[Holland] assembles a cast of characters that exhibit delightful and at times volatile chemistry that feels incredibly natural and satisfying... Louise's prose is lyrical magic."
BOB, *BlueSmokeFire* REVIEWS

"Wow, your book has LOTS of words."
KIRA HOLLAND, AGED 3

THE DOOR

A KALARAAK CHRONICLES NOVELLA
ONE SHOTS SERIES

LOUISE HOLLAND

KIMORI BOOKS

Note from the Author

If *The Door* is your introduction to the world of Kalaraak, welcome!

The Kalaraak Chronicles are a series of epic fantasy stories inspired by my real-life Dungeons and Dragons campaign. This particular novella's concept came not from a specific session at our table, but rather a phenomenon almost all players have encountered: getting stuck trying to open a door.

The Door can be read with no prior knowledge of my other works. If you've already read *Spark of the Divine*, certain aspects of the world will be more familiar, and elements of this story are poised to be of great importance to the Kalaraak Chronicles as a whole. However, I intended for *The Door* to stand on its own while still being indirectly connected to the main novels. So if something doesn't make sense to you, don't worry, it will. Eventually. I hope.

Finally, I feel compelled to mention that I, the author, do in fact know that dolphins are mammals and not fish. This will make sense later. Happy reading.

For every *Spark of the Divine* reader eagerly anticipating the release of the second Kalaraak Chronicles novel — I promise, I'm writing as fast as life will allow me, and I hope this tides you over in the meantime.

KALARAAK
REALM OF EARTH

RALENGRONK

REVELLAND

ONIMA

YMON

SHRIKE BAY

CALMAVEN

KALAC EMPIRE

HAMMERHOLD

GENEBACH

THALRON'S FIRE

THE TRIMOUNT

HIGHPASS

Picking

VENWATCH

LOCH NEROY

GREYWOOD

QUILLKEEP?

HORB'S BEND

TRIVERMEET

VALEFORK

DAMPOU

THE
FREEMERES

BLASHYRKH

BERFORD

ZHURNFELD

DORNOCH COVE

ULVASKER

PROPERTY OF
B. Joyce

CITY OF MIDPORT

AS OF Y53 POST BREACH

CINDERBROOK

RIVER

Halfway Houses

Midport Cemetery

Laughing Sailor Inn

Waterfront District

Noble's District

Merchant's Square

Guardhouse

Fisherman's Wharf

"He who does not carry his home inside
him will be forever a stranger."
Ghassan Kanafani, Palestinian poet

For consideration of entrance into Sigil
Interplanetary Library's Research & Retrieval
Division:
"Mundane Interference & Probability Statistics of
Apostate in Physical Barriers"
Conducted and compiled by Qi Picolas
Submission by Professor Yarrix

Dearest Ms Harkness,

The greatest enemy of all adventurers is, of course, the door.

Though the limitless realms are home to many a formidable foe—cruel, terrifying, often in possession of a ridiculous number of teeth—none has halted an overly eager adventuring party quite like the humble hinged plank of wood. Despite this strange phenomenon's infamy, it remains scarcely documented, possibly due to the embarrassing nature.

Over the centuries, I have noted interesting similarities with our own struggles against the mineral apostate. Namely, its frustrating ability to render even the most skilful Arcane or devout Divine void of magical connection and floundering like a simpleton. The rock vexes me as much in daily life as it does by interfering with our search for the

Architects. I picture apostate as a door of its own, slammed in the face of Arcane ingenuity.

Precious few have attempted to study either occurrence, so you can imagine my delight when the following paper came upon my desk. A student of mine—whether by mere coincidence or great serendipity—conducted a study of both subjects. It took place upon Kalar's first realm, south of the largest continent's capital, and resulted in surprising clarity. I believe my student may have, to use a mundane Kalar term, 'cracked the code' of apostate.

Despite certain... unfortunate events, I consider her research vital to the ongoing retrieval mission. I have submitted her work on her behalf to keep confidentiality of the events intact, and to not draw your ire. I assure you, Miss Picolas has no knowledge of the Architects, Sigil, or indeed any realm outside the seven of her own world, and will remain unaware of just how important her studies may turn out to be.

The ethics of my decision will surely inspire more papers to be written in future centuries, hopefully by another of my brilliant students.

Yours,
Professor Darion Yarrix
Quillkeep Arcane Repository

"The Door"

or

Mundane Interference & Probability Statistics of Apostate in Physical Barriers
(Does apostate block more than the magical?)
by Qi Picolas

Hypothesis: when confronted with a seemingly impossible task, an adventuring party will always find a way around it. This knack for unconventional problem-solving could prove integral to finally discovering an antidote to apostate's anti-magic properties.

Method: I have hired an adventuring party and tasked them with the impossible—opening a door.

CHAPTER 1

QI

Professor Yarrix,

In light of recent events, thank you for your generosity in granting me an audience for my research. I have pieced together what I could from my original notes. Had I known just how much of a disaster this would cause, how many lives I would endanger, I would have abandoned the entire project. I understand if you no longer wish for me to study at the Quillkeep, though I feel compelled to mention my excellent grades and previously spotless record of thirteen years.

"So you want us to... break in?"

The pointed question hung uncomfortably in the hazy tavern air, and Qi Picolas fought the urge to shrink down in her seat. She settled for a quick glance around to double-check that nobody overheard them. She had chosen her venue well—most patrons in the aptly-named Laughing Sailor Inn were too rowdy and intoxicated to be concerned with her conversation.

Now, if only I can get the two in front of me to be concerned with it.

Qi shuffled her stack of parchment away from condensation rings left by the table's previous guests and pushed her spectacles back up her nose. The delicate silver chain keeping them from falling jingled softly in her ear and calmed her nerves somewhat.

"Not exactly," she said. "It's not breaking in if it's my house."

She was awful at lying, but technically, it wasn't a lie. The property *had* belonged to her family... many years ago. Hopefully this crew wouldn't call her bluff. The last group had asked too many questions and left when she gave stuttered, panicked answers, suspecting her to be a city guard or worse.

Qi was flattered by the accusation. She was a scholar, and an Arcane one at that, who stumbled over her spoken words and itched at her splotchy skin when attempting to utter falsehoods. A mole sniffing out Arcanes for the ruling class would at least be confident about it.

"I take it you read my flyer?" she said, trying to partake in some pleasant small talk before the inevitable questioning started. Her guests only nodded, making her feel even more awkward.

Who knew hiring an adventuring party could be so stressful?

When Qi first arrived in Midport weeks ago, she had placed flyers in the markets, the docks, the taverns; anywhere she noticed large numbers of travellers. The discreet advertisement requested a small group of adventurers or mercenaries to complete a delicate task, and promised a handsome reward for it.

Midport was a busy Altaean city by the ocean, bustling with people from all over Kalaraak. A place where those in need of quick coin had plenty of opportunities to earn it. What better place to hire a crew? Naturally, Qi had expected a flood of interest.

Three adventuring parties responded.

Two were proven unsuitable, one way or another.

Now the last group—and her last hope to get this study off the ground—sat at the table across from her, waiting for her to stumble through more details she didn't wish to give. Their hoods were still up despite the late hour, and the dim light from sputtering lantern candles sent shadows dancing across their already concealed faces. Qi squinted through her glasses, trying to stop her imagination from transforming them into fanged monsters under the fabric.

The one on the right seemed to be in charge, although somewhat reluctantly. He was tall and smelled faintly of burned matches, but all Qi could make out of his facial features were his peculiarly light golden eyes that reflected in the candlelight, and his eyebrows, which seemed permanently raised in polite mistrust of her words.

"Your request was purposefully vague," he said. "Why ask for a mercenary crew if all you need is a locksmith?"

"Um, I—"

How eloquent. Perhaps I should write a paper on vocal disfluency and its effect on spellcasting.

"Midport may be a den of chaos," the man added, gesturing around them, "but there are still enough guards about to make law-breaking unwise."

Qi cringed. That was the last thing she needed; the city watch getting involved in her little study and scaring off her adventurers.

"I assure you, no law-breaking is required for this contract," she said hurriedly.

But it *was* encouraged. Another half-truth.

Qi's other guest said nothing, though they seemed constantly on the cusp of speaking. They sat at an odd angle with their back to the wall, an oversized cloak completely engulfing their frame, and their body stayed constantly in motion. Their head nodded along with the music drifting from the tavern's band, and their leg bounced against the ground, keeping the entire table at a slight wobble.

Qi pushed down a twist of seasickness and tried to denote the reason for the movement. Was it anticipation? Hostility? Plain restless boredom? She couldn't tell, and it unnerved her. No amount of Arcane study could help her with reading people. Gods, why couldn't she just be normal?

I don't have to make them be my friends, the logical part of her brain reminded her. *I just have to get them interested in the door.*

"By all means, enlighten us on what *is* required, then," said the man, keeping his arms crossed within his threadbare cloak as he leaned his elbows on the table. The condition of his clothes clashed wildly with the cadence of his voice, which was more Altaean aristocrat than grizzled mercenary.

"It's complicated," Qi began, and regretted it immediately as the golden-eyed man scoffed and pulled his glass closer. The skin on his hands was oddly rippled, like he'd been burned over and over.

"It must be," he commented drily, "since most people do not require assistance to enter their own homes."

"Most people don't have a curse on their front door." Qi's reveal had the effect she intended.

The man froze, glass halfway to his lips.

The other adventurer abandoned all pretence of anonymity and leaned forward excitedly, hood falling back to reveal a heart-shaped face surrounded by masses of dark curls. Pale grey horns spiralled out from above the young woman's temples, curling around like a ram's, disappearing into her unruly hair in places and reemerging in sharp points.

"Ooh, a curse?" the woman said, wide eyes lit up with curiosity as she thrust a hand towards Qi in official greeting. "Now we're talking. I'm Lucky. It's not my real name, but it's what everyone calls me, so you might as well call me that too. Is there a contract? Where do we sign? How much gold are we talking?"

Relief flooded through Qi despite the barrage of questions. "I'm glad I finally got your attention. I should have been asking you from the start." She shook Lucky's proffered hand, a small smile blooming on her face.

At last, some enthusiasm!

Lucky beamed back, showing off a tiny chip in her front tooth and elongated canines. She grasped her companion's arm and squeezed, her long fingernails leaving indents in the fabric and possibly the skin beneath.

"Oh, Trick, can we?" she asked. "I've never worked with a curse before. It could be fun. Please?"

Trick let out a sigh that sounded like his soul leaving his body and removed his own hood, running his hands through dishevelled sandy-coloured hair before rubbing the stubble on his jaw. His pale gold eyes were even stranger in the light. He looked to Qi like if a fairy-tale knight in shining armour were having the worst day of his life.

"Perhaps," he replied, in a tone that clearly said he didn't want to.

Qi laughed nervously, eyes flitting between the two, hoping desperately that they had what she needed so she wouldn't have to go through this again. Her fingers grasped at her necklace for comfort, sliding the odd-shaped amulet back and forth along the chain.

Gods, I am so out of my depth here. I need to focus. What's the most important part?

Qi rummaged through the neatly organised stack of papers in front of her and pulled out a copy of her advertisement. She spun the flyer to face the others and tapped at it nonchalantly—letting her fingers fall onto the smallest line of text, tucked away at the very bottom.

"I hope it was clear that I need someone...*Gifted* to help me," Qi said, choosing her words carefully. Her own spark of Arcane Gift flickered to life within her at the mention, like soothing ice in her veins. "Of either inclination. Do you possess such talents?"

She knew at least one of them did, since Arcanes could sense one another. She wasn't entirely sure why. A side effect of accessing the Weave, perhaps. But she still needed them to confirm it.

Lucky flinched at the question, like she was feeling invisible eyes suddenly crawl over her skin. Trick shifted in his seat absently, drawing his posture taller as if to block her from view.

"I have what you asked for," he said in a voice so quiet Qi had to squint at his lips, "though the very act of asking for it has placed us all in danger. We are too close to Verestead to speak openly of Gifts."

Trick was right. Altaea's intolerance of magic was the very reason she'd grown up across the border, and also why she'd struggled to find any takers for her study. Midport may be a mostly independent fishing town, but it was still dangerously close to the capital, and nobody wanted to risk being ratted out for whatever reward the current king was offering. While the severity of their treatment waxed and waned with the Kingswitch, Arcanes were deeply mistrusted no matter which of the Seven noble families sat on the throne. Being a common-born Arcane in Altaea could easily become a death sentence.

Qi knew that all too well. Her Gift shivered down her spine like a warning.

"Look, I wouldn't ask for... *that*... if I didn't need it," she said, reorganising the already perfectly straight papers in front of her to keep from wringing her hands. "An Arcane problem requires an Arcane solution. Besides, you wouldn't be here if you didn't need coin."

Please. I need *this study.*

Lucky seemed interested, but Trick remained unconvinced.

"Gold might be useful, but you can't spend it in a dungeon," he said. "You have a unique premise, but we have to be practical. Exposing ourselves to the public isn't worth it. Even for what you're offering."

He rose to leave the table. "I hope you find what you're looking for. Good night."

Qi's academic life flashed before her eyes. *This is my last chance.*

"I'll double the payment."

The atmosphere changed.

Qi held in a wince, wishing she could reach out and snatch the words back from the air in front of her. The original reward had been generous already, but *twice* the amount? It was all she had. Years of saving, gone in a blink.

But all the coin in Kalaraak couldn't buy me the experience I'm about to witness firsthand.

Trick's face remained a mask of indifference, but Lucky's sharp intake of breath betrayed just how much sweeter the offer had become. Her hand gripped Trick's arm again, keeping him from walking away.

"Trick," she said softly, like she couldn't believe her ears, "with that much, we could..."

"...I know."

Trick stared down at Qi, eyes narrowed, as if trying to figure out what she wasn't telling them. Even for an Arcane, he was highly suspicious.

Qi held his gaze, refusing to blink, thinking only of exuding confidence and bravery and other emotions she didn't actually have. The picture of a calm and collected employer with no ulterior motive or realm-breaking theories in need of testing.

"Half now, half on completion," Qi said evenly, praying to any gods who would listen that these strangers wouldn't immediately disappear with her gold. "Do we have a deal?"

She kept her fingers crossed under the table.

This is my last chance to see my work become reality.

Trick took a deep breath before seating himself back down. Lucky did not let go of his arm, but this time the squeeze of her hand was gentle. She did it three times before Trick spoke, and his eyes were still on Lucky when he finally gave Qi an answer.

"Fine," he said, in a voice that suggested he knew he would regret it. "Where do we start?"

EXCERPT FROM QI'S RESEARCH

The mineral apostate is Kalaraak's best-kept secret. Despite some deposits pre-dating the Godprison itself, apostate has remained veiled and unavailable to the general public, mainly due to its remote geographical locations and scarcity. Most Arcanes only learn of it once accepted to study at the Quillkeep. Since Arcane users tend to be curious beings, seeking knowledge and uncovering secrets of the realms; that they should endeavour to keep this extraordinary substance hidden is a remarkable feat indeed—and in doing so, have not had their biggest threat used against them by those who wish to quell Arcane Gifts entirely.

Eveka, I know it is highly unorthodox to allow a student to study apostate, but it's been sixty thousand years, we're getting desperate. Miss Picolas remains unaware of its true source. Recent events aside, she is normally very responsible. –Y

CHAPTER 2

QI

Qi barely made it to the house before sunrise.

She hurried along the waterfront docks in the dark, boots thudding softly against the heavy oak planks, repeatedly stifling a stubborn yawn and cursing her lack of sleep. Her expensive new crew had stayed with her at the inn for a time to go over the finer points of their assignment. Trick was overcautious; he asked for confirmation over the strangest improbabilities like he was expecting the building to spontaneously burst into flames.

Qi had given him what little information she could, and made sure both he and Lucky were crystal clear of her conditions; all of which were of utmost importance for her study to be successful.

They had until the following sunrise to break the curse on the door and enter the house.

The door itself was not to be harmed or damaged in any way.

Using any Arcane or Divine Gifts was strongly encouraged.

No, she didn't know how to break the curse.

Yes, she did know what had caused it.

No, she couldn't tell them.

For the most part, they accepted her terms without prying, which was a welcome relief. After studying at the Quillkeep for over a decade, Qi was used to explaining and over-explaining her theories and methods, so to be taken at her word was a little strange. But she supposed all Altaean Arcanes understood how to keep matters of the Weave under wraps, and her crew's personalities took care of the rest. Trick seemed to be even more secretive than she was, while Lucky quickly tired of the technical talk and spent most of the evening making paper rings out of scrap parchment before falling asleep at the table, arms crossed under her head as a makeshift pillow.

At that, Qi called it a night. Her adventurers needed sleep if the 'curse' was to be lifted. She saw them safely out before retiring to her tiny rented room on the inn's second floor.

Qi, however, had not gone to sleep, but instead spent the next hours using her favourite enchantment to transcribe the entire encounter into her field journal. Though the process was agonisingly slow, doing it this way ensured she did not miss a single detail. Every facial expression, every word, even the scents and tastes of the evening would be meticulously recorded upon her parchment without Qi ever touching a drop of ink.

She tried to meditate while the spellwork progressed, but her brain was too wired with the excitement of finally putting her theories to the test.

Thirteen years at the Quillkeep, and I'll finally *be able to prove I'm one of the greats. They'll make me the youngest professor in history after this!*

Qi's enchantment took so long that eventually the gentle hoot of the night's owls gave way to the first feeble squawks of awakening gulls. Though the sky was still wrapped in darkness, she pushed away any last-minute ideas of sleep, deciding instead to head out early and triple check everything was in place.

Qi crossed a small bridge over the river and hurried past warehouses and shipping docks, heading for the odd little residential section left at the very edges of Midport's waterfront district. She avoided eye contact with what few bleary-eyed fishermen or cargo haulers she came across, though they were too busy rubbing their red-raw hands together to notice her. She soon copied them, huffing hot air from her mouth into her stiff fingers. It was *freezing*. Southern winds carried tiny droplets from the ocean to sting her cheeks and dampen her clothing.

Shivering, Qi pulled her cloak tighter around her body and let the edge of manic energy from not sleeping keep the worst of the cold at bay. Fascinated, she watched her own breath become visible in the air before her as if she were a miniature dragon.

To think, I might be used to this weather if I'd grown up where I was supposed to.

Finally, with the ocean at her back, Qi stood outside her family's ancestral home and tried to imagine how it must have looked before.

It wasn't much—a modest wooden building, simple and sturdy, with a high-pitched roof and a tiny front porch. Crammed in beside others shockingly similar, barely an inch or two separating them. Not flashy. Not rich. But in its prime, loved and cared for, it would have stood proudly.

Now it stood empty, abandoned, with rotting wood blocking the windows and dirt and grime covering the sills. If her research was correct—and it usually was—the house had been vacant for almost twenty years.

Qi rubbed her frozen nose violently to quell the sudden urge to cry.

She had no memories of this house. Her grandparents had lost it before she'd even been born for reasons they never spoke of.

Qi knew, though.

She'd spent months poring over records and deciphering terrible handwriting to learn what had become of her grandparents' beloved home.

Three Kingswitch cycles past, a law came into effect banning magic users from owning property. Fearmongering rumours of Arcane manipulation, coupled with the Breach's influx of new gods and

Divines, had sent the Altaean population into a panic. Seemingly overnight, Arcanes went from cautiously revered to hated and feared. The noble houses used the highborn Arcanes in their ranks to flush out the common ones. Before long, it had become an all-out witch hunt.

Qi's family fled the country altogether. This was her first time returning to Altaea, and her first time seeing the house she should have grown up in.

Standing in front of this place still felt like *home*, somehow.

At least I can finally see Mama wasn't exaggerating about the door. It really is beautiful.

The door was a work of true craftsmanship. It was an Arcane technique, but Qi would not be surprised to hear the Maker himself, god of the forge, had assisted her grandfather to craft it. Nestled in the front alcove, the door was arched and sturdy, with wood stained the colour of blackberries and a circular bronze handle. The entire surface was covered in deep grooves, impossibly tiny and gently burned into the wood itself. From the street, it could pass as the wood's grain, but up close, the lines burst to life—becoming vines, flowers, small birds. Telling a story.

A story she wished she could have heard from the crafter himself. But Qi's grandfather had passed into the Silver Stream before her tenth birthday, and what little she remembered of him did not include long talks. He was a kind man, but solitary, prone to long hours shut up inside his workshop and forgetting to eat or sleep until a project was completed. Wholly obsessed with his craft, absorbed in the beauty of creation.

To hear Qi's grandmother tell it, the door was her grandfather's finest work. He spent years upon years perfecting the technique on scrap wood and furniture, and crafted it over months, intending it to be a welcome home for generations. He was an Arcane carpenter by trade.

Before.

Embers of ancestral anger roiled to life deep in Qi's gut.

What a waste—to take someone's home only to have it rot. They didn't even care enough to keep it.

"I'm sorry," she whispered. She wasn't sure if she were speaking to the carvings or to her grandfather's spirit, gods rest his soul, but neither responded. She clutched at the amulet around her neck, fidgeting absently with the clasp keeping the locket closed.

"All right," she muttered under her breath. "Let's make sure you're ready."

Qi stepped towards the door.

Outwardly, nothing happened. If a passerby were to glance in and see her, they would not notice anything particularly unusual. Just a young woman, lost in thought, hand at her chest as if to check her own heartbeat.

But for Qi, moving within the door's vicinity had the same effect as falling off a cliff.

Her connection to the Weave, her calling, the volatile sparkle of magic running through her very soul was suddenly extinguished, and her body tried to shut down. Only years of exposure and training kept her from crying out. Her senses were blinded, her nervous system panicked. Her fingers clutched at her amulet, desperate to ground herself, but even the familiar comfort had no effect.

Qi fought against the overwhelming blanket of black shrouding her that had nothing to do with the dark before dawn and pressed her fingers gently into the wood. Murmuring under her breath, Qi ignored the rising bile in her throat when the simple incantation produced no effect.

Good. The apostate in the door is working.

Qi stepped back.

The rush of Arcane connection filled her with a euphoria bordering on insanity. She laughed aloud, before clapping a hand over her mouth and stifling the sound. The feeling was almost worth the brief torture.

Qi inspected the door thoroughly. If she squinted at just the right angle, she could spot a glimmer of something very thin wedged between the horizontal wooden slats under the handle. Something she herself had added to the door. A substance she'd been trying to unravel the mystery of for nearly a decade.

Apostate.

To a regular person, apostate was just another gemstone; albeit one they'd never seen before, since it was extremely rare. It had a dark amethyst colouring, with veins of black streaking through like lightning. Lightweight, cool to the touch, and quite pretty in the right light. Nothing but a rock.

To an Arcane or Divine, however, apostate was their worst nightmare. It broke their connection with whatever gave them their Gifts, rendering them powerless and weak. It was a miracle the Altaean nobility had not gotten their hands on it.

Qi resisted the urge to stick out her tongue at the rock. Despite being barely bigger than a gold piece, carrying it to Midport from the Quillkeep had been exhausting, forcing her to travel physically despite knowing advanced techniques to shorten the trip. Apostate blocked every type of magic known to Arcane scholars, and none of them had discovered a way to counteract it.

So far.

But Qi had a theory. She believed that the apostate fed on an Arcane's power, and that knowing what it did made it stronger. It was the same as the old adventurer's tale about doors being their greatest opponent; if they expected trouble, they'd manifest it. If they did not, their trials would prove easier to best. Apostate had a physical weakness, a radius that could be exploited, and an unconventional approach would ultimately be its downfall.

In order to support her theory, Qi laced a door with apostate and then hired an unsuspecting Arcane to open it, 'breaking the curse' of apostate in the process. If and how they managed to circumvent the apostate would form the thesis of her study.

Learning how to get around apostate would make Qi not only invaluable to the Quillkeep, but the entire Arcane community beyond it. She would be known throughout all of Kalaraak. Respected. Revered. With enough status to perhaps even rise above Altaea's ridiculous laws surrounding magic use. She would be untouchable.

And then Qi would finally find a way to take back her family home.

EXCERPT FROM QI'S RESEARCH

*Regarding the other main source of magic in the realm;
most Divines have never heard of apostate nor been
exposed to it, and there has been little chance to test
their reactions. Since the Breach some half a century
ago, Kalaraak has seen multiple citizens claiming Divine
power—with that number expected to climb as more freed
gods see fit to bless their most fervent followers with Gifts.
Divines wield magic in different ways to the Arcane,
and at first it was thought both would receive similar
treatment by the general population.*

*However, there is a concerning dynamic emerging
throughout Altaea that places Divines in service to the
ruling class. Rather than subjecting them to harsh laws
and strict training, as they do Arcanes, the noble families
of Altaea placate their fear of Gifts by controlling
Divines with comfort; offering high status and lodging
in exchange for loyalty and their Gifts. One can only
hope Altaea's newest magic users do not lose sight of their
reality—a cage is still a cage, no matter how shiny the bars.*

CHAPTER 3

TRICK

The former Lord Patrick Wicksworth stared out into the cove, watching the morning light dapple on the waves and making a mental list of the things he had given up. It was growing alarmingly long.

He thought little of his family, his home, his title and duties to his House. A minor cost incurred to secure his freedom. He would miss some of his siblings, but it was a big family and most of them were awful—when they bothered to acknowledge his existence in the first place. Trick was used to it. He was the sixth child and fourth son; being overlooked and forgotten was normal. His father, for example, would only notice his absence when winter's chill came to Trivermeet and there was no Arcane to melt the rivers and keep trade open.

Trick glanced over to where the mouth of the Emberbrook river—largest of the three that flowed from the mountains near his home—emptied into the Alsuran ocean. It had taken weeks to follow it to Midport.

Good. Hopefully that meant a delayed pursuit. No, his family would not be missed.

Trick's creature comforts, in drastic comparison, gnawed at him. Selfishness and shame roiled in his belly along with the unfamiliar pangs of hunger. It shouldn't matter, but gods, he missed his cloak. The itchy, cheap fabric of his new-old one set his teeth on edge every time it found contact with his skin. It was a necessary sacrifice; his old cloak, with its soft lining and golden thread, had mostly paid for their passage here.

It had seemed like an easy trade to Trick when he was warm and safe. Now discomfort clawed at his confidence along with the nagging bite of the cold. It was strange for Trick to even *feel* cold—he usually ran way too hot—but here by the ocean water it bypassed his natural heat and seeped straight into his bones.

How do people do this? Live day-to-day without knowing their next meal or bed is assured? How do they find the strength to keep going?

"Tricky?"

A melodic voice called his name, and the corners of Trick's mouth tugged upwards of their own accord.

"Are you going to stare at the sea all day?" asked Lucky, hands on her hips in mock annoyance. "Or are you going to help me open this silly door?"

For a moment, Trick could do nothing but stare at the woman before him. The fuzzy glow of the early morning light made her skin radiate and her ocean eyes sparkle even more than usual. She was too recognisable with her hood back—he should probably tell her to keep it up. But he loved seeing her wild curls loop around the delicate tips of her horns. Yes, she was beautiful, but it was more than that. Looking at Lucky felt like the first gasp of air after being held underwater.

That's how they do it, he thought.

Lucky stood expectantly, still waiting for him to respond. Trick pushed thoughts of soft fabric and warm mead from his mind and rubbed his hands together to chase the odd chill from his fingers. The scarring was less noticeable when he wore gloves, but he'd sold them, too. The world kept demanding gold, and soon all he would have left was his soul. *Seven realms, I should have taken more from the coffer when we ran.*

"Of course I will help," Trick replied, belatedly recognising the question folded within Lucky's gentle teasing. "The sooner it is open and the curse removed, the sooner we may leave."

"Ooh, where should we go?" Lucky said, eyes lighting up with the momentary distraction. "We haven't officially decided. We talked about the Ruby Isles, but are you sure? I do like the idea of being surrounded by the sea. Sun, sand... but that might be too much gold. It's so far away—"

Trick silenced her with a gentle kiss upon her forehead. "My love, after I get this door open, I will take you anywhere you wish. If that is the Ruby Isles, then to the Ruby Isles we go."

Lucky's eyes crinkled with her smile, and Trick was struck by that all-too-familiar twinge in his stomach, like butterflies ricocheting around his insides. Amazement tinged with terror. Yes, he'd won her heart and eventually managed to get them out of Trivermeet, but could he keep her safe here? Anywhere?

Oblivious to Trick's inner turmoil, Lucky mimed rolling up her sleeves. "Then let's break a curse."

Trick pushed the worry of a thousand unknown variables to the part of his mind reserved for when he was trying to sleep. He had a job to do. Open a door.

If the door is even capable of opening. There has to be a catch. The Arcane girl offered us way too much gold to believe otherwise—especially if she herself could not break it. But I must remain optimistic, for Lucky's sake.

Together, Trick and Lucky approached the small home. The house in question looked perfectly normal and uncursed; merely dilapidated and damaged in a mundane manner. It matched the rest around it, with boarded windows and a thick layer of dust.

Trick knew little of Midport—only that it was the best way to leave Altaea in a hurry—and to him, most of the architecture here looked the same. Wind weathered wood, thick and well-oiled to keep the water out. He wouldn't quite call their current location the slums, but it definitely wasn't home to nobility. Anyone with coin wouldn't live downwind of noisy cargo ships or a fishing wharf. The foreign scent of saltwater and seafood refused to leave Trick's nostrils no matter how hard he tried to burn it out.

"The entire area must have been abandoned," mused Lucky as she fished a crumpled piece of parchment from one of her many pockets. "I wonder why?"

"I don't know, but it's fortunate for us," Trick replied. "The last thing we need is an audience."

"This is definitely the right place." Lucky squinted at her own cramped handwriting. "Qi said it was the one with the—oh, look at the door! It's gorgeous! How would you even do that?"

Trick allowed himself ten seconds to admire the door's admittedly impressive carvings, but he didn't let his mind wander. He needed to solve the problem, then leave before the next one caught up.

"All right," he said, rubbing his stiff fingers together. "First, we need to check the back and the windows before we assess the door itself. Figure out what we're up against. The curse could be nasty. Who knows what it does?"

Qi could not even speak of it. Gods, it could render us deaf or mute or unable to think, it could trap us in place, it could—

Lucky nodded, then bounded for the door, fingers outstretched towards the bronze handle. "You think too much, Tricky."

Trick sighed, trying not to laugh, before Lucky's high-pitched shriek of terror sent fire coursing through his blood.

Trick reached out and yanked Lucky backwards, searching wildly for the source of her fear while his own flared. His Arcane Gift—if he could call it that—roared to life in subconscious defence. Trick tried desperately to keep control of the flames attempting to burst from inside him, pushing Lucky behind him to distance her from himself as much as the door.

"What? What is it?" Trick asked.

Lucky did not answer.

The heat within surged again.

Finding no enemy, Trick threw everything into calming his fire before it consumed him. He exhaled slowly, ignoring the thin plume of smoke that escaped his lungs, and held his breath until the flames within him settled to their regular embers. When the pale smoke had dissipated from around him, he pulled Lucky to him, tracing his hands up and down her arms in comfort and searching her face for answers.

"What happened?" Trick repeated, keeping his voice soft.

For the first time since they'd been introduced, Lucky seemed unwilling to speak. She pointed a shaking finger at the door before burying her head in his chest.

Trick gritted his teeth. He wasn't entirely used to being brave, but loving a woman like Lucky required him to dig a little deeper than he was comfortable with.

Time to see what the curse was about—and why it needed an Arcane to break it.

Trick approached the door the way he would a rabid animal—with extreme caution. More from habit than true need, he grazed his thumbs across his fingers, sending tiny sparks scattering towards the ground beside him. Occasionally there was a burst of light, and heat radiated from within his hands momentarily as flame caught from the casual movement. Trick's only trick, as it were.

"Be careful," warned Lucky.

"I always am," Trick replied. "It's what got me into this mess in the first place."

He was rewarded for his quip with a rather unladylike snort, and a wry smile stole across his face before he could help it. He knew Lucky was thinking of the same thing he was—the very first night they had officially met, where he'd warned her to be careful around the manor path's uneven cobblestones and then promptly found himself tripping over one.

The mirth left quickly when Trick came within arm's reach of the door. He crumpled to his knees, a strangled cry wrenched from his lips.

The winter chill soaked through him instantly. He shivered violently and pulled his old-new cloak tighter around him, disgust at the fabric overruled by the need for warmth. His teeth chattered together and his fingers ached, the overlapping scars standing out even more as the rest of his skin flushed an angry red. In his entire life, he had never once felt this cold.

The fire inside him had gone out.

Trick was Arcane, he'd been born with the fire. He didn't know another way to be. The absence of his heat was so debilitating it was like his body had forgotten how to function. It was all Trick could do to cradle his head in his hands, holding in a scream while his insides turned to ice.

It was Lucky's turn to drag Trick back into the safety of the street. Once they passed an invisible point, the curse lost its grip and Trick's fire bloomed once more in his chest. His connection to the Weave sputtered like a lone candle in a storm wind before burning brightly again.

For the first time in a long time, Trick was grateful for his Gift.

Warmth flooded his body as sparks flew from his fingers, which he'd been frantically rubbing together in an attempt to force his fire to appear, and he almost set his own cloak alight. Tears pricked at his eyes, though from terror or relief he did not know. He was unsure if he could stand. The sheer nothingness the cursed door had brought upon him... it would haunt him until his dying day. Trick had no words for such a horrifying experience.

"Well, that sucked," said Lucky.

Trick choked out a laugh, cupping Lucky's face and wiping the tears from underneath her own eyes. "Have I ever told you how I love your way with words?"

"Once or twice," she replied, giving him a proud smile. "I think it was the first time we spoke, actually. Something about my mouth? You were quite charming."

Trick laughed again, shaking his head. "You and I view that conversation very differently."

For Trick, Lucky's arrival into his life was like being shaken awake from a nightmare. His father had often raged about how House Wicksworth needed another Divine to serve Trivermeet, but he could never have imagined such an enchanting woman on his doorstep. It had taken weeks for him to work up the courage to try to talk to her, and longer still before he managed it. In the months that followed, he orchestrated moments for their paths to cross, to steal time together between their separate duties—and later, their escape. It had only worked because he planned it so carefully, down to the second.

But he'd done it. He was out in the world, as far away from his home as he had ever been, searching for a way to properly disappear forever.

Now the only thing keeping them alive and free was gold, and it was rapidly running out.

"Well, I thought you were very sweet," said Lucky. "You were the first to make me feel truly welcome at the manor. Your words were kind, even if you did stumble over them a bit."

"I don't even recall what I said," Trick replied. "All I remember is my heart pounding so hard I was sure you'd hear it. I didn't know what god you served, after all. What if you'd been there to replace me?"

Lucky's face twisted in amusement. "Me, play with fire? Please." She kissed the tip of his nose before getting to her feet and offering him her hand. "The only fire I like is yours."

Trick's insides smouldered happily. Why were they here again? Gods, she was mesmerising. It was no wonder he'd thrown his life away for this precarious new adventure.

He let her help him to his feet and spent a few more moments holding her, making sure the last of his fire was burning completely within his control. Though he was never truly in danger of misting—using too much of the Weave and burning out permanently—he couldn't afford an outburst here. It would be a dead giveaway for his father to know where they'd been.

His father. The Archduke of Trivermeet was sure to have noticed Lucky's absence by now, if not his own. But how fast would their disappearances be pieced together?

Lucky dusted off her dress. "Well, now I've seen a curse, I'm not so excited," she said, eyeing the door with newfound caution. "I guess I thought it would only be cursed for Arcanes. Serves me right."

Trick made a vague noise of agreement, already lost in thought. It intrigued him, how the curse also blocked Lucky's connection to her Divine power. Perhaps that could be the key to undoing it.

As an Arcane, Trick understood little of the nuances surrounding Divines and their returned gods. The Godprison had only been breached for fifty years, and many of the new-old gods remained unknown to the general public. Divine magic seemed unbalanced to Trick—some Divines, like the one his father first invited into their house before he was born, wielded healing abilities so strong she could pull a man back from the brink of death. He'd heard stories of Divines to warrior gods who could fight for days without tiring and whose weapons never missed.

Others, like his beloved, seemed content to simply feel connected to the strange magic flowing through their veins. That was also a foreign concept to him.

"It's too bad we can't just take the curse with us," Lucky said wryly. "Your father would never be able to track us down."

Trick was jolted back to the present with an unpleasant reminder of his current predicament. He breathed out hot air and willed his Gift to keep to a simmer. Careful, always careful. Solve the problem in front of him before the ones behind caught up.

"No more stalling," he said. "We've got a curse to break, gold to collect, and a ship to board."

Lucky gave him a playful salute. "We'll be out of here in no time."

EXCERPT FROM QI'S RESEARCH

To understand the properties of apostate, we must first consider what it does not *do. Apostate is no physical deterrent; though a single piece of great size could withstand assault, most shards crumble easily under simple blunt force. It cannot block intentions, either; whilst it may sever a Divine's innate connection to a god, apostate cannot prevent the physical act of prayer.*

Furthermore, apostate is limited by its own radius, with potency varying with the size of the crystal. Only small shards have been recovered for study, though there are rumours of massive deposits in unexplored areas of the Kalac desert. Would, say, a piece the size of a building render magic there unusable for miles?

Chapter 4

TRICK

Lucky's optimism was usually enough to sustain them both. But as the hours passed, the unease smouldering within Trick only grew.

Nothing could budge the door. Any idea was explored, no matter how outlandish.

They tried chants from children's nursery rhymes to ward off evil.

They tried holding hands and pulling each other out of the curse's radius.

They sat at the stoop, miserable and shivering through their lack of connection, hoping their bodies would somehow absorb the curse and allow them to transport it somewhere else.

Trick choked down his mounting frustration and meditated, searching his mind for anything that could possibly help. Qi had said magic was the answer, but no magic could penetrate it.

Lucky spent hours praying to her god, the guardian of the waters, and was eventually rewarded with a visit from two strange-looking beasts Trick had no name for. Swimming right up to the docks, they made odd whistling noises and sprayed water out of their backs into Lucky's face, who seemed delighted by the attention. But ultimately the creatures served no purpose other than a brief distraction from their mounting failures.

Many of their conversations followed a similar pattern. Suggestion, hope, trial, failure. The repetition and constant disappointment began to wear on Trick's already frayed nerves, but he tried to focus on Lucky, who never seemed to run out of ideas—though they were becoming less magical and more criminal in nature.

"Could we just pick the lock? Maybe the curse is on the inside."

"Do you know how to pick a lock?"

"...I was hoping you knew."

The only glimmer of accomplishment came when Trick lit a candle and then approached the door, expecting the flame to go out, but it stayed burning merrily. It didn't matter that the fire had come from Arcane means—once it took physical form, the door considered it identical to any flame forged by flint. Trick latched onto this information, lighting his fingers over and over again, trying to find something that would allow not just *a* fire but *his* to exist in the curse's presence.

He met only dead ends and extinguished flames. With each snuff, his hope fell further into darkness.

Lucky poked around the waterfront district's neighbouring harbour, hoping to find somebody who could shed some light on the curse's origin. But what few sailors or cargo workers she managed to charm into talking with her had no useful answers. She stomped back to the door, pouting, before gathering her skirts behind her and sitting on the dock, letting her legs dangle toward the water.

"Any new information?" asked Trick absently, still experimenting with the stubborn candle. "What did you find out?"

"Where do I start?" Lucky replied, digging through her satchel for a hunk of bread she'd had stashed in there for days. She ripped into the stale loaf with a huff and pointed down the docks at different people in turn, little more than moving shapes now from this distance.

"Lionel over there," Lucky continued, "has been hauling crates onto galley ships for over forty years, but he's thinking of retiring soon because his back makes awful noises whenever he picks anything up now. Mr Peregrine is planning on asking the barmaid at the Laughing Sailor to marry him—I think he really likes her, his ears turned the most interesting shade of pink every time he said her name. Sybil inherited her fishing fleet from her father, and she and her wife pull in twice the catch of any other in all of Midport. Honestly, good for them."

Trick chuckled, making the mundane flame of the candle in his hands jump. "Your way of getting people to open up to you is a Gift all of its own."

Lucky sighed and leaned backwards, gazing up at the cloudy sky. "But when I asked them about these homes, they all clammed up," she continued wistfully. "Most I could get was that Arcanes used to live here, and it's bad luck to even walk past the houses now. I guess they all moved away after the silly law changes. Can you imagine? Having to leave your home because of your Gift?"

Trick paused, a new twist of shame joining the embers coursing through his body. He knew about the decree banning magic users from owning property, but it pained him to admit he had never truly given it much thought. He was an unimportant member of a very important family; a House of the Seven, the highest form of Altaean nobility. His father would serve as King of Altaea soon, just as all the Archdukes did when their time came. He grew up in a sprawling manor attended by servants, he wore fine fabrics and ate fine food. Trick, despite being Arcane since birth, had never once questioned if there would be a roof over his head.

Until now.

Which is why we must leave Altaea, he reminded himself. *Lucky dreams of a house by the sea, and she will have one, even if I have to build it with my own hands.*

Lucky went quiet, which in itself was strange enough to break Trick out of his concentrated state. He blew out the candle and sat beside her on the dock, staring out at the waves without really seeing them. The logical part of his brain urged him to get back to his task, to keep trying to break the curse on Qi's door before their time was up.

But Lucky was uncharacteristically sombre, and it worried him. They could spare a few minutes.

Lucky's dark hair spilled around her like a cloud of ink staining the dock's wood. Trick brushed aside an errant curl swaying into her vision, tucking it behind her ear. The silky strand glided through his scarred fingers and he tried not to cringe at the difference. Everything about her was soft. She deserved better than a touch as coarse as his.

Stop, he thought, mentally shoving down his own insecurities. *She needs you.*

Trick let his eyes wander over Lucky's face, taking in the tell-tale signs of her bottled-up apprehension. A muscle in her jaw twitched as she clenched it repeatedly, and the edges of her nail beds sported tiny crimson wounds from her picking at the skin around them. She swore and jammed one finger in her mouth, having ripped the side too much.

"Lucky," Trick murmured, taking her injured hand in his own and kissing it, "I can practically *feel* you holding the floodgates back. Tell me what you're thinking."

"It just makes me... sad," said Lucky finally, cheeks flushing with the confession. "How they had to leave their homes. I don't know what to do with the sadness. I can't help them come back, can I? What can I do? I feel helpless. And then I feel angry about feeling helpless, and then sad again."

I've never seen her so disheartened, Trick thought. Perhaps the curse affected more than just their magic.

"It is unfair," he said. "I wonder why Qi would even want to live here, curse aside. Many Altaeans still act like being Arcane is contagious."

"They're weird about Divines, too," said Lucky. "I never noticed before, but it's getting hard not to. I thought serving in a House of the Seven would be wonderful, but honestly, Trick, the only good part was you."

She sighed again, louder this time. "Why does it even matter which god someone believes in? There's plenty who don't worship at all, and the gods don't mind. Divine, Arcane, mundane, we're all still just... human. Why is everyone so afraid of anything different?"

"I don't know, my love. People fear what they cannot control. That includes others, I suppose."

"Well, they shouldn't," said Lucky, a spark of indignation igniting on her face. "I just think it's funny how..."

Lucky began rambling, letting all that was pent up inside of her come rushing forth like a waterfall of words from her lips. She talked at length of the unfairness of the anti-Arcane laws, flailing her hands in an animated fashion, and expressed her outrage at the dilapidated state of the houses behind them when there were plenty of Midport citizens sleeping on the streets. She questioned the treatment of Arcanes and Divines alike. She even had the courage to speak ill of his family—of which he was quite proud, considering how intimidated she had been by his father.

Trick let her rant, idly stroking her hair, captivated by the passion bursting within her. It was one of the things that had first made him fall head over heels for this strange girl who'd turned his life upside down. No noble in the Seven's courts spoke with half as much conviction.

He didn't quite know what to say, or indeed when to say it, since Lucky rarely paused to take breaths. So he simply listened. It seemed to be all she needed, since before long her slender fingers found his again and intertwined, and her smiles became genuine once more.

"I'm sorry, Tricky," she said, sitting up and leaning her head against his shoulder, careful not to let the tip of her curled horn pierce the fabric of his awful new-old cloak. "I got really gloomy there for a minute."

"Don't apologise for having feelings," he replied, wrapping an arm around her. "It makes you real. You don't have to be happy every moment of the day."

Lucky snorted. "I usually am," she replied, winking at him. "You have yourself to thank for that. But I'll be even happier once we're as far away from Altaea as possible. Let's get back to working on that."

She jumped up, invigorated and full of optimism once more, and bounded back towards the abandoned house.

Privately, Trick envied her ability to shake off what troubled her so easily. He had never been the type to work through his feelings aloud—he was more adept at pushing them down inside until they couldn't reach him. The niggling unease at still not having solved their problem prickled through his mind like shards of ice, and his control slipped as the fire within rose to combat it.

Struggling to keep calm, Trick exhaled slowly and blew a stream of grey smoke from the side of his mouth, angling it away so Lucky didn't notice. This place had already stolen enough of her unbridled joy; he couldn't let her see how much their lack of success was weighing on him. It was his burden. It would do no good to weigh her down, too.

The fire inside him quietened, but the feeling remained. Like he was slowly running out of air.

Lucky eyed the cursed door, her eyes sparkling with the glint of a fresh idea. Trick took shallow breaths as she explained it and hoped it would be the one to finally see them triumphant, all the while ignoring the rising sense of dread creeping over him.

Lucky's idea didn't work.

Neither did the next one. Or the one after that.

The knots in Trick's stomach wound tighter. Kindling for the fire.

"What if I broke a window? I could crawl in."

"And shower us both in shattered glass and rotting wood?"

"Right. Plus Qi would probably be upset with me."

The day became overcast and threatened to rain, while chilled winds blew out their testing lanterns and reddened their cheeks. When they took breaks, Lucky tucked her hands within the folds of Trick's clothing and warmed her icy fingers on his skin. He flinched and yelped in protest only because it made her laugh. The truth was, he adored it. Both the touch and the fleeting regularity in his temperature.

"At least we're not on a ship right now in this wind," Lucky joked. The icy salt air whipped her hair around both of their faces as if in agreement. "We'd be frozen to the mast and you'd have to burn it."

Trick could barely smile. They *should* be on a ship. They should be miles away already, and it was his fault they weren't.

Lucky experimented with what little physical power she could control, but unsurprisingly, getting the door wet had no effect. She lamented the newness of her Gifts and her inability to wield them as the weapons or tools needed, but Trick reassured her over and over that it didn't matter. He could never tell her in such words, but Lucky's Gifts were for showing appreciation to her god, not solving problems. Lucky did not even know her god's name. Although Trick believed them both to be much stronger than she herself knew, the fact remained that her control over water was fragile in nature, and her Gifts would not help to open the door.

Trick had known from the beginning that this was his curse to break.

An Arcane problem required an Arcane solution.

Trick resorted to reciting every lesson he'd received in the Arcane training academy his father had dumped him in as a child. A grim place that may as well have been a prison. Of course, the nobles of Altaea would not describe it as such; to them it was a boarding school designed to hone—or repress—as much of an Arcane's talents as possible. Noble-born Arcanes were taught to control their Gifts, not explore them. Once they showed prowess in one element, one specialisation, the others were abandoned.

Trick was no illusionist, enchanter, or tinkerer. He knew only fire.

And fire is not going to open this damned door.

Trick knew Lucky was counting on him, that she believed he could solve the mystery of the door. But could he? Or was his inability to break the curse simply proof of what he'd always suspected—that his usefulness as an Arcane, and his value as a person, only reached as far as his flames?

EXCERPT FROM QI'S RESEARCH

So where does the myth of the adventurer's door fit in to this study? Contrary to apostate's properties, a door blocks only the physical—and yet can prove a formidable obstacle to all types of magic user, since a line of sight is so often required for even simple feats. A door can prove an Arcane's undoing just as easily as a mundane adventurer, especially one who has come to expect magic to solve their problems.

CHAPTER 5
TRICK

The would-be cursebreakers continued their futile attempts until nightfall. The stringy winter clouds marred any vision of the twin suns setting, but the sudden drop in temperature made it near impossible to continue. Lucky used her icy breath to imitate Trick's smoke, earning a weak chuckle, but Trick's spirits were becoming harder and harder to lift.

At Trick's insistence, Lucky headed back to their room at a rickety halfway house when the witching hour arrived with no change to their situation. Perhaps she could return with fresh eyes and spot what they had missed. He loathed the idea of her being alone in an unfamiliar city, although the no-nonsense attitude and meaty arms of the six-foot-tall Revellan proprietress who had given them a room kept Trick from fearing for Lucky's safety.

Lucky, of course, had no idea that the large woman stood guard outside her door, but Trick was grateful despite both the extra gold it had cost him and the general unfriendliness of the inn itself. It was grimy and unpleasant, but it was cheap, and Lucky would be safe.

He still walked with her across the bridge and back into the city, the resolve to return to his task threatening to crumble as her bright eyes reflected in the lantern light. His hand left hers more reluctantly than ever. He promised her he would join her when he could, but he had to go back.

Back to the door. Back to the living manifestation of all his failures.

Trick traced his fingers along the lines of the door and wished desperately that he could somehow burn it down without destroying it. He would even go so far as to risk misting himself, if he could. At least if he died defeating the curse, Lucky would still be entitled to the reward, and he could pass through the Silver Stream into Requiem knowing he had guaranteed her freedom.

It was a futile thought. The curse would not allow a single spark of his Gift; there was no chance of misting even if he wanted to.

Trick could not admit defeat, but the last hours of night leached what little confidence he had left and tossed it into the watery abyss at his back. There was no way around it. Every time he stepped too close to the door, the flame within him sputtered and died. It was as if the door itself repelled magic. He supposed that was why Qi, with raw Arcane energy radiating from every pore, had not been successful in lifting it.

Why she thought anybody else had a better chance was still lost to him.

"Godsdamn you," Trick muttered, rocking back and forth just outside the curse's reach and watching his fingers reignite over and over. The flash of heat stung every time, though he was long past feeling pain in his hands.

Sleep tugged at him, but he refused it for as long as he could. He splashed cold water on his face and pinched his own skin to keep lucid. He *had* to break the curse on the door or they were as good as back in Trivermeet under his father's iron fist. But his optimism had long faded, especially without Lucky's cheerfulness to replenish it. Here it was, the first real test of his independence, of his ability to take care of them both, and he was watching their foolish dream evaporate in front of him.

Trick did not return to the inn. He couldn't stand to see the pity in Lucky's eyes if he crawled into bed beside her defeated.

By a door, of all things.

Leaning up against the door, Trick drifted in and out of a fitful sleep that brought no rest. All the while, the last minutes of his free life ticked treacherously by.

There was only one small consolation—the curse could not reach his dreams.

As he slept, Trick began to burn.

Their time was almost up.

Trick had tried everything, and still the door remained cursed. He sat with his back to it, leaning against the intricate wood carvings, staring out at what little of the ocean he could see in the darkness. He was used to the emptiness of the curse by now. Perhaps it was how he should feel, since he had failed to beat it.

Lucky reappeared at the docks just before sunrise, shouldering both their bags and dark circles under her eyes. Trick couldn't bring himself to look at her. He groaned and banged the back of his head against the awful door. Gods, what was he going to do?

"Trick," said Lucky gently, "you need sleep."

"What I need is to open this godsdamned door," Trick muttered. "Besides, that was our last night at the inn. I'd sooner sleep here than give them another gold piece for that hay pile."

Not that I have any left to give, he thought darkly.

Lucky sighed, dumping the biggest bag off her shoulder onto the ground with a thump.

"I know," she said. "I swear it had fleas. I could barely sleep—the owner kept stomping up and down the hall outside my room all night. And they tried to charge me for the bread they left on the table when we first arrived! Can you believe it? It's *complimentary bread*. I laughed in their faces." She giggled again, reliving the altercation. "What are they going to do, rip it from my belly?"

How could she laugh, when they were so close to losing it all? How could he doom them to a life where she never made that sound again?

Lucky's smile faded as she regarded him. "Tricky..."

"I can't do it," Trick said quietly. "I can't break the curse. I can't open the door."

Lucky pursed her lips, searching for words. Trick knew she would try to cheer him up, to excuse his mistakes and soothe his fears. But this was not something words could assuage, and he did not deserve to even hear them. A storm of despair—bigger than just his failure to cure the curse—was starting to build inside him, and he was too exhausted to contain it for much longer.

Lucky began her attempt. "It's all right—"

"It is *not* all right," Trick said, cutting her off, shame bubbling under his skin, like his flames were boiling his blood despite the curse's disconnection. "If I cannot open this door, there is no more gold. Without gold, I cannot get us out of here before someone catches up. Gods, the guard is probably already in Midport by now. You think Father will just let us go—let *you* go?"

It stung to admit the truth, even to himself. His father wouldn't care that Trick had absconded, only that he'd taken House Wicksworth's newest Divine with him. What a fool he had been to think they wouldn't come for her immediately. Trick raked his hands through his hair, panic bobbing in his throat and threatening to choke him.

Lucky forced him to stand, though she cringed as the curse cut off her Divinity. The numbness of the door and the cold made Trick's stiff limbs protest. She tried to pull him away from the door, but it was like his legs had turned to lead and he could not will them to follow her. He watched her fingers leave his grasp with a nasty sense of foreboding.

"So... so we'll just give Qi back her gold and find a new job," Lucky said hesitantly. "An easier one—"

"I can't," said Trick, pressing his fingers into his temples violently. "That gold went to getting us out of Midport. I already paid them. We're supposed to be on a ship tonight."

Lucky paced back and forth, spluttering out more half-baked plans, more ideas they'd already tried, but her voice was starting to sound muffled through the ringing in Trick's ears. Gods, he'd messed it all up, and now what would happen to them? They'd be dragged back to Trivermeet, prisoners of the grand estate he once vowed to see burned rather than return to.

Trick leaned against the door for support. The emptiness of the curse started to feel like the only thing holding him together.

"We don't have to go to the Ruby Isles," said Lucky. "I don't care where we go. Anywhere near the sea is fine, Trick. Let's just go."

Trick only shook his head. Despite his desperation, Trick's honour would never allow him to abscond with Qi's gold, even if it could help him escape his fate of returning to Wicksworth manor. He'd be confined to his room this time, isolated and alone, only allowed to surface when something needed Arcane flame.

Nothing but a human flint striker.

And Lucky? She'd be reduced to worse—a court jester, performing carnival tricks with Gifts given by a god she'd never be free to serve properly. What a waste of a Divine's life, all so the Wicksworth name weighed more heavily in the Seven's opinions. What a waste of *her* life.

I've doomed us both.

"Trick," said Lucky carefully, skirting around the edges of the curse's vicinity. "Please come here. I don't want to feel it again."

Trick leaned with his back against the door, panic clouding his mind. He stared at Lucky—the beautiful, wild, carefree love of his life—and was unable to think of anything other than the tragedy loving him had brought upon her. A Divine of the sea god, landlocked.

At least I'll still be able to see her from my window, he thought selfishly.

A sickening realisation shocked the fog from Trick's brain.

His father wouldn't allow them both to stay in Trivermeet. Not after this defiance. His father would blame Lucky for Trick's runaway thinking, for his transgressions; would accuse Lucky of bewitching him. An echo of his father's voice taunted him.

"You've been acting rather strange since that girl arrived, Patrick... Do I have cause for concern?"

"Trick," Lucky's brow furrowed with worry. "Get out of your head."

But Trick knew his father. The Archduke Wicksworth hated magic, like most mundane men did, and viewed the users of it as barely sub-human. Trick's Arcane Gifts were tolerated because they were useful and he was family.

Lucky would not get the same treatment.

Her status as a Divine was only desired because of the esteem it provided the family, and even that had been overshadowed by their disdain of her unconventional race and questionable level of skill with her Gifts. They knew she came from nothing. She would not be missed by anyone other than him.

Trick looked into Lucky's ocean eyes, currently full of love and concern for only him with no second thought for herself, and a shiver ran down his spine that had nothing to do with the cold. Horror coursed through him like wildfire.

His father would get rid of her.

"Tricky, talk to me."

Perhaps permanently.

"Forget the stupid door. We can find another way."

There was no other way. Trick had failed to lift this curse, failed to open this damned door and earn the gold that would buy their freedom, and in doing so he had possibly condemned the woman he loved to die. Trick buried his head in his hands, groaning, inwardly scrabbling like mad to escape the well of utter desolation he'd spiralled into, searching desperately for a scrap of hope, of *something*...

But all he found at the bottom of the pit was rage.

Seven realms, I've been bested by a godsdamned door.

Trick's scarred hands curled into fists as he eyed the door, pure fury building inside him. It wasn't fair. How could a simple door keep him from getting to live a quiet, safe life away from his wretched family? How could a plank of rotting wood deny him the only thing he'd ever wanted? How could a stranger's curse cost him the only person who loved him for who he was and not the fire he loathed?

"Trick, say something," said Lucky insistently, fingers latching around Trick's arms and shaking him. "Do something!"

"I can't!" he shouted, the words sounding more like a howl of misery as they ripped from his throat. "I can't do anything! I can't solve riddles or build houses or break curses. I can't escape what I am. All I do is destroy everything in my path. I can't save us, I can't save you! All I do is BURN!"

Lucky yanked him towards her, intending to pull him into an embrace, but as Trick's body left the curse's influence, the heat inside him returned with a surge so strong he almost blacked out.

Every tiny spark, every crackling flame born of anger and fear and repressed by the curse came rushing back at once. His body burned white-hot and wrenched a scream from his cracked lips. He'd tried to push it down for too long, tried to stamp it out and smother it while it did nothing but build inside him.

The Arcane fire within his soul became a relentless force pushing on his every nerve, demanding to be released.

He could no longer contain it.

His Gift exploded.

The last thing Trick remembered was pushing Lucky away as hard as he could before his own flames consumed him.

An unexpected side effect of apostate was discovered during this experiment. When an Arcane's connection is repressed, the intensity of their power risks magnification should they still be concentrating on it when removed from apostate's vicinity. There is no recorded deliberate use of this phenomenon, though I dare say replication attempts will be made in future. Extreme care will need to be taken to safeguard against accidental misting. Mistings—when an Arcane exudes an extreme amount of their power at the cost of their physical body—are all reported to be fatal.

Chapter 6

LUCKY

There was a rush of sound, before a murky, eerie silence.

Lucky opened her eyes and blinked furiously, confused by the blurred surroundings before realising she was underwater. The cove wasn't deep, but the heavy skirts of her sodden dress dragged her down within seconds. Lucky held her breath out of instinct and tried to reorient herself, kicking her legs furiously but finding no purchase.

Pushing dark clouds of her own hair from her vision and flailing her arms wildly, she searched for the way up, but it was pitch black and freezing cold and she was still winded from hitting the water. Her boot caught in a large clump of kelp, trapping her leg. Forgetting where she was, Lucky screamed in frustration, a stream of angry bubbles escaping her mouth and disorienting her further.

Help, she thought desperately. *Help me!*

There was a whooshing noise, a flurry of movement, and suddenly Lucky's body propelled through the water at great speed. Her head broke the surface with a gasp, but she didn't stop—launching out of the water, she sailed through the air and landed unceremoniously back on the docks with a loud splat. Groaning and coughing up seawater, Lucky glanced back at the waves, now gently illuminated with a golden glow. Had she been underwater long enough for the suns to rise?

The two creatures her god had sent earlier made odd clicks and whistles in the water below, obviously very proud of their quick actions. Their sleek grey heads bobbed in and out of view, giving them the appearance of living buoys.

"Thank you," Lucky said breathlessly.

They squeaked happily before disappearing back under the water.

Lucky's head spun with a hundred thoughts at once. She'd never been good at sorting through them. She wished for a moment the weird fish would stay, that her god could stay and help her. She wasn't very good at using her Gifts. She'd been brought to Trivermeet to serve in their House as a Divine, but she could tell they'd been disappointed at her lack of physical manipulation—she could barely water plants. The sea was her favourite, but she'd needed a home, so why wouldn't she accept the offer? Honestly, the Archduke should have just taught his children how to use water as well as fire, and then he wouldn't have needed her in the first place. But then she would never have met Trick...

Trick! Where was he?

"Trick!" Lucky tried to shout, but it came out hoarse and bubbly. More water splattered onto the dock.

Lucky shook her head, trying to clear her ears and get her bearings. Hair was plastered to her face and tangled in her horns, sticking to her skin and driving her mad. Racing thoughts all interrupted one another, making it hard to focus. Everything was hazy. She could barely remember which house they'd been tasked to uncurse, and the paper in her pocket was sure to be ruined. Nothing looked familiar. Maybe she'd washed up at a different part of the district?

But then the wind changed and the acrid smell of smoke hit her nostrils, and Lucky became acutely aware of why it was so easy to see her surroundings.

The suns had not yet risen.

The entire waterfront district was now on fire.

The blaze had erupted quickly, as all fires do, and the feast of kindling before it only made it hungrier. Flames flickered in different colours, dancing bursts of lavender-blue and sea-green among the orange caused by years of salt soaked into the wooden buildings. Lucky was momentarily mesmerised—it was her favourite thing for Trick to show her; the pretty changes in flame depending on what fuelled it.

Now a rainbow of destruction spread wildly across the abandoned houses, reaching across the rooftops with fiery tendrils like fingers reaching to crush the homes it descended upon.

Lucky's instincts screamed at her to run, to get back below the water where it was safe.

But I have to save him.

"Trick!" she yelled again. "Where are you?"

There was no answer, but through the cacophony of cracking beams and roaring flames, she thought she could hear screaming. Her heart lurched. *It has to be him.*

Lucky whipped her head around desperately, searching for assistance, but the city still slept—it was mere minutes before daybreak. A few alarmed cries and shouts of warning floated across the cove from early dock workers, but they were distant. It was too dangerous. The fire was already completely out of control. Plumes of toxic smoke barrelled into the sky. Heat poured off the structures and flushed her face.

Nobody was coming to help her.

She had to do this herself.

Lucky sent a silent prayer to the sea god and plunged into the blaze.

Running down the dock, Lucky shrieked as pieces of burning buildings cracked and collapsed beside her. She screamed for Trick even as the smoke cooked her lungs from the inside and made it hard to choke out words. Orange tendrils reached for her from skeletal window frames as she ran past them.

Wasn't this what Trick was afraid of, what he'd warned her about, why he'd pushed her away again and again until finally letting her love him? He was always so careful, so controlled—all the while he lived in fear of his own Gift. For the first time, Lucky understood his hesitancy to allow her close, despite knowing his love for her had sparked long before their first spoken words.

The cursed house was not thirty feet in front of her, but she could barely see for the smoke. It tasted like acid and stung her eyes, forcing tears to stream down her face. Pulling the collar of her wet shirt over her nose and mouth helped to breathe. Lucky dodged partially collapsed roofs and burning debris as she approached the house with the cursed door, her usually scattered mind occupied by a single thought.

Where was Trick?

Lucky almost collapsed in sheer relief when she found him. Trick stood frozen, right where she'd left him, his clothes singed and smoking and his cloak alight. The fire did not discriminate; it burned its creator as harshly as anything else in its path.

The door stood stubbornly behind him, a beacon, and the area around it burned slower despite the flames licking at the frame. Trails of scarlet embers traced paths in the carvings of the door's surface, making the designs glow and flicker as if they were alive. The door should already be cinders—maybe the curse offered it more protection than the mundane wood around it, or maybe the fire was too focused on Trick to consumed the door behind him.

Lucky didn't know, and right now she didn't care. All she cared about was the burning man in front of her.

"Trick," she said hoarsely, "we have to get out of here!"

Trick was catatonic. He stared into the flames like they had hypnotised him, murmuring under his breath, his brow knit in quiet horror. His body glowed like embers simmered under his very skin, rippling and distorting the air around him. It was so bright it hurt her eyes.

"Trick, look at me!" Lucky shouted. "Wake up!"

Trick didn't respond. He swayed slightly as she ripped the burning cloak from his body, stamping on the fabric in a feeble attempt to staunch the flames, but otherwise he made no movement. She couldn't tell if he even knew she was there. Desperate, she slapped his face, before swearing and shoving her fingers into her mouth instinctively. The slightest contact with Trick's skin blistered her own.

Gods, I can't even touch him.

Lucky hovered her hands over his face, pleading with him, trying to force him to look at her. Finally, his brilliant golden eyes found hers. There was no moisture in Trick's body to cry, but his eyes were rimmed red and full of warring pain and sadness.

"Lucky," Trick mouthed, the sound barely leaving his lips, "go."

"No," she said, sobbing.

"Go," he insisted. "You can still get away."

Lucky knew he wasn't talking about the fire.

"I can't leave you."

"Just let me burn," he choked out. "Go and live."

But would it be living without him?

"Trick," she whispered, tears streaming down her face, "I want you to come with me."

The exact words she'd used the night they'd finally decided to run away. He'd been so insistent she get out, but he hadn't planned to join her until she asked him to. Typical, self-sacrificing Trick. Never once taking his own wishes into account. Believing he deserved to suffer simply because he was different.

The flames clawed closer. Soon even the curse would not hold them back.

"Please," said Lucky. "Please come with me."

Indecision flickered in Trick's eyes, but his body didn't move. Couldn't move. He stayed in front of the door, the light framing him as if it were his own funeral pyre. Trick's body glowed brighter, pulsing, the raw energy from the Weave cooking him from the inside. He would let himself burn for her, even if it cost him his life. He couldn't let go of what his fire made him.

But I can't let go of him.

So Lucky did the only thing left she could think of.

She threw herself at Trick and wrapped her arms around him.

They crashed backwards, Trick hitting the cursed door and almost breaking it off its hinges. Even the curse could not contain the heat from his body.

Only the seawater drenching Lucky's clothes kept her alive, even as it turned to hissing steam and scalded them both. The air radiated with heat, warping her vision. The flames crackled louder.

Closing her eyes, Lucky braced herself to burn. She would rather die here with Trick than spend the rest of her life remembering him in these last terrifying moments. She tensed, expecting flames to engulf them both, but it didn't seem to be getting worse... if anything, Trick was cooling down. Lucky lifted a glistening hand and tilted her head, fascinated.

The water wasn't from her clothes, it was from *her*.

It's my Gift. It's keeping me safe. Helping us.

Lucky pressed her body into Trick's, willing the water to envelop them both. Most of it bubbled and evaporated away, but the cool sensation of running water stayed across her skin and protected her from the worst of the heat. A light, peaceful ocean breeze wound its way through the smoke to ruffle her hair and cool her face.

Lucky buried her head in Trick's chest and prayed harder than she had in her entire life.

The contact shocked Trick out of his stupor. He tentatively placed his arms around her, and the sizzling of hot meeting cold drew an involuntary gasp of relief from his lips. Lucky stood on her tiptoes and pressed her own against them, hoping it would be enough to bring him back to her.

"I love you, Trick Wicksworth," she whispered. "I'm not afraid of you. You're the only person I've ever known who's held me with gentle hands."

She grasped the sides of his face, silently begging him to look at her, to see her past the fire burning in his golden eyes. Drops of water from her fingers washed away some of the ash, leaving the skin underneath clean. The fire couldn't have him. He was hers.

"You can't hurt me," said Lucky firmly. "But you have to stop hurting yourself."

Trick melted into Lucky's arms, sinking to his knees when their combined weight proved too much for her to handle. Lucky focused on drenching them both with the water still coating her skin. Trick choked back a dry sob as she ran her hands through his hair, over his face, letting the water soothe his scarred skin. She kissed him over and over, the taste of salt water dampening the smell of smoke.

Somewhere between the whimpers of pain, Trick sighed.

"We have to go," said Lucky, pulling at Trick's hands. Could he walk? He could barely stand.

Lucky eyed the burning door, suddenly grateful for whatever strange magic kept it intact longer than mundane wood. This house had stayed standing longer than she would have guessed, but it could still crumble any minute. They had to move back to the water. She didn't think her newfound Gift would be enough for much longer, especially since she didn't have time to explore it. Escaping the blaze was now their top priority. Her body fatigued, her mind exhausted, Lucky could think only of getting them both to safety.

I can't lose him now. Not after everything we've done to be free.

Trick gave a weak noise of agreeance, but he was still barely lucid. Lucky propped him up, doing her best to support them both, and was about to start hauling him to the docks when she heard it.

Trick's murmured apologies and the menacing crackle of the flames were drowned out by a new sound.

Screaming.

Unfamiliar screams. High-pitched and terrified.

And they were coming from the wrong direction.

Lucky stared at the cursed door and the burning house beyond it in horror, the realisation seeping in through her waterlogged mind.

There was someone inside.

EXCERPT FROM QI'S RESEARCH

Elemental affinities are most common among Arcanes, manifesting young, yet without proper training these powers amount to little other than bursts of energy. Unschooled Arcanes are unlikely to possess the discipline to perform even basic incantations or enchantments.

However, apostate's main weakness is that while said elemental manipulations are Arcane in nature, the resulting effect is indistinguishable from its mundane counterpart. While it cannot be conjured within apostate's radius, if the effect begins elsewhere, apostate is powerless to stop it. Rain still falls, ice freezes, lightning shocks.

And fire burns.

CHAPTER 7

LUCKY

True hysteria gnawed at the edges of Lucky's mind now, tearing her in different directions while keeping her feet rooted in place upon the porch. They had to get to safety. She had to save Trick, save herself. They were seconds away from being burned alive.

But she could not abandon a stranger to die.

"There's someone in there!" she shouted against the roaring of the flames. "We have to help them!"

Trick shook his head, not in disagreement but seemingly to clear the spots from his eyes. He was still burning; his mouth and nose spewed thin plumes of pale smoke on every exhale, though she could tell he was trying to hold his breath to stifle it. He reached out to the fire with scarred fingers, but the flames did not recede. Despair spread across his face.

"I... I can't control it," he said. "It's not mine anymore."

"I'm going in."

Trick reached for her, trying to push her towards the docks. "Lucky, you can't," he choked out, still wrestling with the burning inside of him. "Even if we could get through that godsdamned door, the chances of getting to whoever it is are basically nonexistent."

Trick's eyes said what he dared not voice. He couldn't let his fire claim her life.

But we can't let it take anyone else's, either.

Lucky choked down the fear bubbling to the surface and flashed Trick a false smile of bravado. It didn't feel like her genuine one, but it still had the effect on Trick it always did. His gaze softened, like he knew she'd already made her mind up and he'd resigned to follow her anyway. A rush of affection for him made her suddenly giddy, and Lucky laughed aloud from the sheer ridiculousness of the emotion given their current circumstances.

"It's all right," she replied, this time with a real smile. "I'm lucky, remember?"

Trick sighed in exasperation, but his eyes lost some of their hollow look and he stayed with her. Together they approached the cursed door, which was finally beginning to burn in earnest. The blackened wood creaked as the embers raced across it. Still beautiful, even as it succumbed to the flames.

Lucky didn't have time to stop and think. She ignored the curse completely and threw herself into the door. Her damp hands curled around the bronze handle and yanked as hard as she could.

The door opened.

Their magic had kept them from discovering the simplest answer of all.

It was never even locked.

Deciding she could be annoyed about that later, Lucky barrelled through the door. She winced as the curse tried to rip her Gift from her, but even the blanket of numbness was not enough to stop the comforting ripples coursing over her skin.

"Come on," she yelled.

Trick followed close behind, cursing and trying to shield them both as ash and soot rained from the roof. Together they crashed into the house, desperately searching through the smoke for any signs of life. Lucky shouted over and over, hoping against hope that whoever was trapped inside could hear her.

"There!" said Trick, pointing into a room that might have once been a kitchen. "I can sense someone!"

Lucky climbed over collapsed beams, dodging flames and coughing intensely as the smoke invaded her lungs. She rounded a corner and gasped.

A strange, misshapen glass sculpture took up the whole room. Glittering and glistening, warping their own reflections before their eyes. Even as she watched it changed shape, melting with the heat before shooting another spike towards the ceiling. Rivers of freezing water ran down the sides. Lucky pressed a hand to its surface and sighed in relief as her burned fingers made contact.

"It's ice!" she said.

A cocoon of ice, protecting an Arcane. If Lucky squinted, she could make out the shape of a person crouched within.

They weren't moving.

"You have to melt it!" said Lucky.

"What if I just make it worse?"

Trick's hands were shaking so badly he balled them into fists at his side. The smoke escaping his nostrils had turned a darker grey. Lucky had seen that look before. He was terrified to use his Gift.

"Look at me," said Lucky, grabbing his face. "This is what your fire is for. You can still control it. You can make this right."

Trick nodded, setting his jaw, then thrust his hands onto the ice. Steam hissed like a horde of angry snakes, billowing into their faces. Soon Trick's hands sank into the ice, creating divots, and he held on as long as he could before wrenching his frozen fingers out. Lucky kicked the place Trick had weakened. The ice cracked from the pressure, splintering and sending shards cascading onto the floor to be swallowed up by the inferno. Soon they made a gap large enough for one of them to fit.

Lucky squeezed inside the makeshift barricade and found Qi Picolas.

The Arcane girl was curled up in a ball, surrounded by parchment paper and ink bottles, frozen fingers clutched around her amulet. Her face was deathly pale and her glasses were askew. It looked as if she'd used everything she had to summon the wall of ice before passing out.

Lucky placed a hand on Qi's chest, frantically checking for a heartbeat. Relief coursed through her as a steady thumping pulsed underneath her palm.

"She's alive," Lucky called to Trick, willing her voice to stay steady. "But we need to get her out right now."

Lucky braced herself and dragged Qi towards the gap. With Trick's help, soon they had the unconscious girl on the other side of the ice. Propping her up between them, they hobbled back the way they had come, deathly flames licking at their heels as they struggled with the uneven weight of a third person. Qi stirred, realised she was being helped, and tried to go back the way they had come.

"My... my papers," Qi protested, disoriented and trying to pull herself to proper consciousness. "My research. Save–"

She cut herself off in a choking cough, the blackened smoke around them thick and making it near impossible to see. Lucky gripped Qi's arm, still thrown around her shoulder.

"We've got to save you first," she replied.

Qi stopped struggling long enough for Trick to keep guiding them towards the entrance. Lucky prayed the whole time that it would still be open when they got there.

Finally, they reached the cursed door, which was now hanging partially off its hinges. Qi made a small, strangled cry before losing consciousness once more. Trick hauled the Arcane girl's limp body through the door, narrowly avoiding the white-hot frame, and behind them Lucky tried to scoot past it. But a falling beam caught the edge of the wood just as she passed beneath. Her shoulder slammed into the door, breaking the final hinge.

A great chunk of wood from the top of the door, little more than charcoal now, broke away and crashed around her.

Lucky screamed as hot ash clung to her clothing, burrowing through fabric until it reached the skin beneath. The scent of burning hair singed her nostrils and she brushed embers from her curls frantically, panic rising so high she wanted to scream until her lungs gave out. The fire finally encompassed the door entirely, a curtain of flames blocking her path.

The water sent by her god streamed over her like a waterfall, whispering words of comfort she might have imagined through the haze of pain.

Just keep going.

Lucky gritted her teeth and launched herself through the fireball.

EXCERPT FROM QI'S RESEARCH

Why does the door prove such a formidable opponent to adventurers? Perhaps it is a refusal to see what is in front of us, or a physical reminder of our limitations. Or, just maybe, encountering a closed door triggers a self-fulfilling prophecy. For when people are forced to pause and think about who they truly are, they believe they will fall short of what it takes to step through, and instead relish the opportunity to blame their failures upon external circumstances rather than their own actions. It is a brave adventurer indeed that chooses to find a way through—and in doing so, may find that the door itself was never the obstacle.

Chapter 8

LUCKY

Against all odds, she made it out.

Collapsing onto the dock, Lucky coughed until her lungs burned and she thought she might throw up, but through gasping breaths she managed to keep her meagre lunch down.

Qi was not so lucky—the Arcane girl had properly awoken only to lose whatever her stomach contained, retching over the side of the wharf into the water below. Lucky felt bad for the fish that had to swim through it. At least the dock was deserted. Hopefully that meant any others had escaped in time. Lucky refused to consider the alternative.

By now the entire waterfront district was ablaze. The fire had spread inwards, tearing through the abandoned homes and moving to warehouses and storage facilities. It was so bright it might as well have been midday. Sparks and embers filled the air, carried by the wind and landing on rooftops across the river, setting even more houses alight.

The multicoloured flames reflected in Trick's pale eyes, somehow even more otherworldly with the rest of his skin blackened by ash. He stared at the burning buildings as if seeing fire for the first time, horror etched in his expression.

"Gods," he whispered. "It could take out all of Midport."

Lucky stood, brushing the ash from her skirts. Breathing hurt, but she kept trying.

"You have to stop it, somehow," groaned Qi, barely able to sit up. One of the circular glass panes in her spectacles was shattered, giving her eye an odd splintered effect. Her bloodless face and shaking hands showed what she could not say—that she couldn't help. She addressed Trick, but Lucky didn't mind. What could her own Gifts do against an inferno this size?

"I can try," said Trick, wiping some of the sweat and ash from his brow. "But I can't do it alone."

He was rubbing at his fingers again, absently creating tiny sparks. He always did that when he was worried. Lucky gently took his hands within her own and kissed them right on top of the worst of the scars. He sighed again, his burned hands soothed by the current gently coating her skin. His fire calmed by her water.

Lucky was struck by sudden inspiration.

She and Trick were such an unlikely pair, opposites in every sense of the word. Their upbringings, their experiences, their Gifts. But instead of clashing, they balanced each other out. When she was too meek to stand up for herself, when she was drowning in uncertainty or frozen from indecision, Trick helped her. Fought the battles she couldn't. Kept her safe. In turn, when Trick burned—whether from his Arcane gift or his intense self-loathing—only she could douse the flames and bring him back towards the light. Maybe an Arcane problem didn't need just an Arcane solution after all.

Maybe there *was* something she could do.

"Lucky you're not alone then, are you?" said Lucky, giving him as big a smile as she could muster. It hurt, too. Her skin was aching. "You've got me."

Trick laughed, a bleak chuckle tinged with exhaustion. "Yes. Lucky."

She wasn't sure if he was agreeing with her or simply saying her name like a hymn, as he so often did. What mattered was that he believed in her. That was all she had ever wanted.

Qi pulled herself together and left for somewhere slightly safer, directing any people she came across to evacuate the area, while Lucky dragged Trick to the edge of the waterfront. There she explained her idea, which was more of a feeling than a true idea, but she asked him to trust her anyway—silently hoping against hope that it would work.

Of course, Trick agreed, despite the fact that to fail would doom them both. He would do anything for her.

They stood back to back; Trick staring down the fire, Lucky facing out into the ocean she loved so much. If she squinted, she thought she could still see her weird fish friends bobbing in the waves on the horizon, their tails waving back and forth in distant greeting. Her heart swelled. Her god had not forsaken her when she needed it most—the only difference now was how she wielded her Gift.

Purposefully.

Not to amuse stuffy nobles by filling decanters and tending to extravagant gardens in the hot sun. No, she was meant for more than that.

Wasn't she?

Lucky grabbed Trick's hand and intertwined her fingers with his own. Sudden doubt crept in, whispering that her plan was ridiculous, that it could never work, that the entirety of Midport would burn with her failure. Uncertainty swirled in her mind like a storm, making it hard to think.

"Tricky, I'm scared," she whispered. "What if it doesn't work? I don't even know my god's name. I've never asked this much of my Gift before."

Trick squeezed her hand three times. Their secret language. *I love you.*

"Only because you've never needed to, my love," he replied softly. "You're Lucky. Maybe they were saving it all for this."

Lucky reached out to the water and pulled.

Every inch of her being called to it. Every prayer, every thought, every whisper she'd ever sent out to the water in her life, asking it to return to her. To help. The current running over her own body paused its rippling, giving her the sensation of being submerged. Her waterlogged hair hung limp, her eyelashes heavy with stray drops that blinked into her eyes and risked breaking her concentration.

Lucky emptied her mind of everything but the way the water became warmer on her skin where she held Trick's hand and sent a desperate plea to her god—or perhaps to the ocean itself.

Please, she thought. *Please help me save them.*

For a heart-wrenching moment, she felt nothing.

Then came a horrendous sucking sound, like a drain gurgling, and the breath ripped from Lucky's lungs as the water seemed to syphon from the docks in front of her.

Moving away, towards the horizon.

So much water receded that the bottom of the cove was visible. Fish flapped clumsily on the wet silt, debris from the fires or careless dock workers lay exposed on the sand below. The Emberbrook river slowed to a trickle. Distant onlookers pointed from the other side of the cove, shouting in dismay. It was as if the water itself was deserting them.

The sense of dread inside her rose.

Trick groaned as he strained towards the fire, calling it, trying desperately to control the uncontrollable. Lucky whispered what reassurance she could, trusting in their connection to carry the words to him amid the roaring of the fire. Trick's Arcane Gift was strong, stronger than he would admit to himself, and only by embracing the part of himself that burned would he ever achieve true control over it. He stood taller with her encouragement, and though the flames struggled against his call, Lucky felt heat at her back and knew at least some of them were responding.

It was both a blessing and a curse. They would save the rest of the city, but soon the inferno would be upon them once more.

Even the water from Lucky's skin came free to join the retreating seawater, droplets flying through the air and leaving her more damp than wet. The heat surged behind her. For a single moment, despair washed over her, but she squeezed her eyes shut, clung to Trick's hand like an anchor, and kept pulling desperately, stretching her fingers out towards the ocean.

She had to trust in her faith, trust in her Gift.

Trust in herself.

I can do this.

A tremendous rumbling shook the ground beneath her feet. Lucky opened her eyes and gasped.

All of the water was returning to her at once.

It took the form of a tidal wave, fifty feet high, so tall it crested over the tops of the buildings before them. Distant onlookers, drawn by the fire and deaf to Qi's protests, now turned and ran from the giant wave—fleeing for their lives as the immense wall of water rushed towards them. Shouts of terror were soon drowned out by the rumbling of the approaching wave.

Lucky braced herself and held her breath. Roaring filled her ears.

The water hit the land with an explosion of sound and covered the entire dock. Lucky fought the urge to scream as the wave pounded against their bodies, spinning her around and threatening to wash them right back into the burning, but she held tight to Trick's hand and stood strong.

The water knew her.

It wouldn't hurt her.

She took a deep breath and invited the ocean in.

Seawater raced through her, clearing her lungs of ash and smoke and rushing through her veins until it was like she *became* the ocean—she was drowning, but she could finally breathe. She embraced the wave, letting it run over her, the cool touch calming her senses and freeing her mind of all its runaway thoughts. No insecurity, no fear. There was only the cleansing of the water.

Lucky kept her free hand outstretched, a cry of sheer determination wrenching from her lips as she manipulated the water. The wave twisted, reaching the very edges of the blaze, covering the flames while avoiding the parts of the cove still inhabited by Midport's most concerned or reckless citizens.

The rushing water encased her and Trick in a wall of soundlessness, and for a moment it was so quiet Lucky could hear their heartbeats. She usually couldn't stand stillness, but this was almost peaceful.

Trick, his part in the rescue complete, wrapped his arms around Lucky and gently held her against the continual battering of the water rushing past. Though she knew her control would keep them both safe, Lucky was grateful for his support. She could do it without him, but it was better together.

That's what love is, she thought with wild clarity. *Holding on through the high waters.*

There was a great sizzling sound; like the fire was screaming as the wave smothered it. Hissing pockets of burning air warped Lucky's vision. The burning buildings were blanketed, the roaring of the water dousing the shrieks of the fire. Clouds of smoke and steam billowed into the air, and the scent of the salt in the water mingled with the acrid smell of burning wood.

Lucky kept pulling at the water until every ember was subdued, until the last spark of flame quenched. She might have imagined it, but it almost felt like her unnamed god was there with her, a guiding hand atop her own, helping her navigate the unfamiliar power that had always been swirling deep inside of her.

Finally, the fire was quelled. The water retreated, its task complete, and soon the ocean returned to a state of sparkling stillness. Lucky sent a simple prayer out to her god, imagining the white crests of the waves as applause for her use of her Gift.

Thank you.

Her wall of water no longer blocking her vision, Lucky took in the aftermath of the wave. What she saw stole her breath away.

The entire waterfront district was completely drenched. The twin suns broke through the clouds to send tentative rays of winter sunshine to sparkle on the wet buildings. Blackened, skeletal frames of some burned houses still stood, partially crumbling from the fire's assault and the battering of the wave, dripping with seawater. Others were washed away completely, leaving behind nothing but piles of rubble or empty plots of land.

There was so much damage—rivers of soot drained along the sides of the buildings and plumes of smoke still choked the air. One pier still stood, the damage minimal, while the other now lay at the bottom of the cove. Warehouses were gutted and collapsing, and stray planks of splintered wood drifted into the streets, carried away from their original structures by the retreating water.

It was a catastrophic mess. Midport was badly scarred, possibly forever.

But it was no longer burning.

The people were safe.
Lucky fell to her knees.

EXCERPT FROM QI'S LAST NOTES

The Arcane fire and subsequent Divine tidal wave inflicted upon Midport during this study resulted in damage to upwards of fifty buildings, mainly those situated in the abandoned waterfront district. Although a number of injuries were reported, mostly by wharf workers and civilian attempts at healing; the disaster miraculously recorded zero fatalities. This is likely due to Lucky's ability to redirect her water, Trick's eventual containment of his fire, and my own mundane efforts to evacuate bystanders.

Perhaps when I present my findings to Professor Yarrix, I will be able to use my actions during the disaster to offset the severity of having caused it in the first place.

CHAPTER 9

QI

In the aftermath of the fire, Qi stood on the threshold of her family home.

Or rather, what was left of it.

The door was gone.

It was like the air had been sucked from her lungs. Staring at the void where a beautiful piece of her grandfather's history should be hurt just as much as losing him. All her recent experiences faded into the back of her mind—the fear of the fire, the battering of the tidal wave, the exhaustion at feeling her Gift run dry, risking a misting just to stay alive as the house burned around her.

None of it compared to the raw pain that tore through her now.

Tears streamed down her face and into her neck, leaving tiny rivers of clean skin amidst the blackened ash. She couldn't stop imagining the looks on her grandparent's faces if they had been alive to see it, disappointment and grief coating every line on their faces. They were already blurred in her memory, most of her recollections fuzzy and faded. The permanent dull ache of their loss ripped open anew. This place was all she had left of them, and now it was gone.

And it was her fault.

Qi fell to her knees in the charred remains of the door and wept.

I should never have tried to do this. Now I've destroyed the only home I felt alive in.

She should have returned to the inn yesterday after checking the apostate was secure, but the old bronze key kept safe in her amulet was practically singing to her. She'd just *had* to see if it still worked.

Walking into the house felt like being a ghost—tiptoeing through rooms she would have grown up in were it not for ridiculous laws born of pure greed and misplaced fear. In a trance, she had poked through drawers and wardrobes, searching for anything her grandparents might have touched. Folded-up pieces of parchment with ink so faded she could not read the words. Chipped glasses and mismatched plates in the back of a cupboard. An empty vase. Most of the furniture was still there, covered by motheaten sheets and a thick layer of dust. The speed with which her family had been forced to flee broke her heart all over again.

It didn't matter what a piece of paper said. This was her *home*.

Qi couldn't bring herself to leave, even when the suns rose and her adventurers came to break the curse she manufactured. Besides, Qi needed to stay close to record how they solved it. That was what she had told herself, anyway.

Qi relived the last hours over, trying to pinpoint a moment where she could have saved it all. Her spellwork had taken too long again. She'd fallen asleep too late. Maybe if she had slept sooner, not been so drained by her enchantments, the smoke would have woken her up. She wouldn't have been caught off guard, racing to protect her work...

It doesn't matter now. It's all gone. And I'd trade every single word to see this door whole.

Her frantic searching throughout the burned house had resulted in finding only charred scraps of parchment. Her research was unsalvageable. She would have to start again. Qi wondered vaguely if she should feel more upset about that. But the pain of seeing her life's work in ruins paled in comparison to the overwhelming grief that threatened to undo her.

Qi could do nothing but cry in front of the door.

She didn't know how long she stayed there, knee-deep in ash and debris, sobbing until her lungs felt like fire and her eyes turned swollen and red. Every time she started to get a hold of herself, a new thought would send her reeling with a fresh wave of tears.

How could she ever face her own mother again? After destroying the childhood home she'd hoped to one day return to?

"I'm sorry," Qi said, the words catching in her throat. Who was she even saying it to? Her grandfather? Midport? The door itself? She had too many apologies. Even Trick and Lucky—as much as Qi wanted to blame them for the destruction, part of her knew the awful truth.

This never would have happened if I hadn't brought apostate here.

Qi's eyes wandered aimlessly, taking in the destruction before her without really processing it. She couldn't see very well through the crack in her glasses. She found the old bronze handle, still glowing slightly from the immense heat, and took great care to avoid touching it. Only a single piece of the door's wood had survived the worst of the flames. It was no more than an inch wide and blackened at the edges. Qi reached for it, sniffling, and tried to inspect it closer through her tears.

Most of the intricate Arcane carving had been destroyed. Only a single line was still clear, but it was enough to recognise what it was supposed to be.

A flower.

Qi squinted, the outlines of the petals pulling an old, fractured memory to the surface of her mind.

River lilies. Her grandmother's favourite. Of course, her grandfather had included them.

The realisation brought on a fresh wave of agony, and Qi sank lower to the floor, cradling the tiny piece of broken wood in her hands. She wanted to curl up and die right there—perhaps then she could offer her grandfather a proper apology when her soul arrived in Requiem, the realm of the dead. His proudest work... her family's legacy... reduced to charred rubble. Even her Gift couldn't soothe her, though subconsciously she tried, contorting its icy river to flow through her veins in an attempt to cool her—

Wait.

Qi gasped through her tears, breathing in the smoke and almost choking. She dove her hands into the powdery cinders in front of her. Frantically, she searched, hissing as hot ash burned her fingers, wincing as stray splinters pierced her skin, brushing it all aside until...

There it was.

The apostate. Right in front of her.

It can't be.

Qi reached for the dark material, fingers trembling. The heat of the flames and subsequent wave of frigid water had damaged the delicate crystal, but there were still a few decently-sized pieces buried in what remained. Qi turned a shard of apostate over in her hand, her thumb sliding over the unusually smooth surface.

Trick's fire—or perhaps Lucky's water—had transformed it.

The obsidian veins that ran through the gemstone now glittered with an almost liquid quality. The amethyst shined brighter, more transparent than before. It caught the light and twinkled merrily, sending a purple sheen onto the ashen ground below.

Qi brought the apostate so close to her nose it almost touched her skin and bumped her glasses. Normally, the proximity would make her vomit, but it only brought an odd, muffled sense of peace.

Her magic was still connected.

"Seven realms..." Qi whispered.

The scholar in Qi took over as she held up the gemstone to the light. It was alien and unnerving, but it was undeniable. The apostate had changed. What was the exact cause? The fire may have been created by Arcane means and doused by Divine, but the elements themselves were indistinguishable from mundane occurrences. Did that make a difference? Either way, the experience had removed the outermost layer from the rock, exposing an even deeper mystery within.

Inspiration struck.

With shaking hands, Qi removed her broken glasses, then dug through her satchel until she found the required components for a simple enchantment—a familiar one she'd used way too many times before. Once she was properly prepared, to be certain, she moved the tempered apostate so that it was right in front of her.

I have to know I'm not imagining it.

Qi took a deep breath and attempted to repair her glasses.

Murmuring quietly, Qi moved her hands in a delicate pattern, like she were braiding strands of fabric through the air before her. Her Gift sputtered a little, like it too was unused to the presence of the strange mineral, but it still responded to her call. The familiar ice in her veins still sang, and the magic still coursed through her. Long, thin trails of the Weave flowed from her fingertips, glittering in brilliant turquoise, illuminating the air around her and lighting up her face with an otherworldly glow.

For the first time in a long time, Qi allowed herself to marvel at the beauty of the Arcane. After spending a decade sequestered at the Quillkeep, surrounded by other magic users, she'd forgotten what a miracle it was.

The cracks in the pane of glass slowly sealed, shimmers of ice-blue sparks sinking into the grooves until they were smooth once more. Her mended glasses glowed with Arcane energy before settling, indistinguishable from before they'd shattered. Qi held them up and squinted through them. The world came into focus, and the first thing she saw clearly was the apostate.

Her enchantment had not only worked, it had worked perfectly—while in apostate's direct proximity.

Qi was so shocked she started laughing. The sound echoed in the empty house, reverberating her own giddiness around her.

"I can't believe it," she whispered to herself.

This changes everything.

Qi attempted to clean her newly-repaired glasses so she could study the apostate closer, but every inch of her clothing was still covered in soot. She placed the piece of apostate in front of her and paced back and forth, muttering simple incantations and testing against its old radius.

Soon, she had identified the main difference—and it was nothing short of incredible.

Instead of cutting her off from the Weave entirely, the tempered apostate let her *inside* the bubble of anti-magic void it created, leaving her Arcane connection muffled but intact. If she concentrated hard enough, Qi could *feel* the apostate's own magic pulsing slightly, coexisting with her own. Running over her body like a current. Like an invisible blanket, draped around her shoulders by an older relative.

Like a shield.

"I can't believe it," Qi repeated.

The grief of losing the door, of her family home, still ached within her, but now the edges of the pain were rounded. It had not been for nothing.

As Qi grasped the apostate in one hand and the last tiny piece of the door in the other, a pleasant shiver ran through her body. A feeling she had not experienced for a long time.

The excitement of a new discovery.

EXCERPT FROM QI'S LAST NOTES

Apostate is a curious substance in that it is both highly detrimental and surprisingly useful to Arcane practices. In its natural state or discovered without warning, it wreaks havoc upon Arcane and Divine power alike, but it can also be utilised in Arcane training. Traditionally, pieces no larger than coins have been used to help control Arcanes attempting volatile or unsafe enchantments, but until now, nobody had thought to include the effects of elemental conjuring upon the apostate itself.

When a minute quantity of apostate is tempered, however, it can be used instead to temporarily repress an Arcane's outward connection to the Weave while leaving their innate abilities intact—and therefore, conceal their true nature.

CHAPTER 10

QI

Hours later, Qi sat in a secluded corner of the slightly damp and seawater-scented Laughing Sailor Inn, scribbling furiously onto the parchment before her.

She'd lost most of her notes to the blaze, and it was imperative she save the memories of the event. Her Gift thrummed inside her happily despite the tempered apostate concealed beside the key inside her amulet, but she dared not use her scribing enchantment in such a public setting.

Soon, she would leave Midport for the safety of the Quillkeep once more, to present her research and plead her case against the disaster it had caused.

But for now, methodically and with great care, Qi compiled her findings.

If used correctly, she wrote, *tempered apostate shards could hold the key to not just safely studying dangerous and volatile forms of Arcane magic, but also returning displaced Arcane refugees to their rightful homes lost in the law changes of King Ascendant Ashbourne in 28P.B. Since the tempering appears to need both the fire of an*

Arcane and the water of a Divine, the process will be
difficult to replicate, however—

"Qi?"

Qi did not stop writing as someone approached
her table, but she glanced up when she realised
she still sensed the Arcane energy emanating from
them. Interesting. She would have to make a note of
that, too. Despite the cramping in her hand, part of
her relished the process of handwritten notes. She'd
been scribing via enchantment so long, she'd almost
forgotten how accomplished she could feel to fill a
page with her own writing.

"May we join you?" asked Lucky hesitantly,
half-hiding behind Trick.

Qi nodded absently, looking up only long enough
to be polite. She was still thinking of how best to word
her next sentence.

In their brief moment of eye contact, Trick gave her
a tight-lipped smile. His sombre eyes were brimming
with regret.

"We are so sorry," he said, helping Lucky into the
chair opposite Qi before pulling up a chair from a
neighbouring table. He wore no cloak, and his shirt was
rolled up at the elbows despite the chill temperature. He
should have been shivering, given the circumstances, but
Qi supposed after facing down an inferno it would be a
relief to feel the cold. The rippled, scarred appearance of

his skin did not stop at his hands, though the burns on his forearms looked much more recent.

Lucky clutched a bouquet of slightly wilted flowers, likely all she could find after the fire sent most of Midport's traders into closure for the day. Qi tilted her head, the fragrance transporting her back in time. Lilies.

"I thought we were all going to die," said Lucky quietly. "I bought these for you. I know it doesn't help... Nothing could... oh, Qi. I don't know what to say."

Qi dotted an 'i' with more vigour than needed and thought about shouting, or crying, or demanding they leave. But none of those actions felt like the right thing to do.

"You don't have to say anything," said Qi, sighing. "Nobody could have predicted what would happen. It's not your fault."

She wasn't sure why she had already decided to forgive them. Perhaps it was the scent of the river lilies clouding her senses and making it hard to hold onto the anger. It could be the passage she'd just completed in her notes; detailing how Trick and Lucky had turned her down until she bribed them with more gold, and even then they had seemed more resigned than excited. How they continued to try and solve the unsolvable until it consumed them, because they were desperate to leave Midport and lacked the funds to do so.

I deceived them with the apostate. I cannot punish them for giving all they had to break a curse that didn't really exist.

Lucky started to cry. Trick wrapped his arm around her, rubbing up and down her shoulder in comfort. A simple movement Qi had grown up seeing every day. She blinked, clearing the vision of her family from her mind. Something within her shifted.

As Trick offered further apologies and increasingly unrealistic ways to compensate her, Qi looked at the two would-be adventurers in front of her and truly *saw* them for the first time.

Lucky was glistening, droplets of water clinging to her skin like morning dew and mingling with the tears on her face. Her hair was even wilder than when they'd first met, almost completely concealing her horns and curlier than ever. She still smiled, but she clutched at Trick's forearm whenever he wasn't speaking, like she needed to make sure he was still there.

Trick was calmer in Qi's presence than their first meeting, and the angry redness of his burned arms didn't seem to bother him. But he kept glancing towards the inn's door like he was expecting unwanted company. He had the haunted eyes of a hunted man—or perhaps the lover of a hunted woman.

They both still reeked of smoke despite the barrage of the wave cleaning most of the ash from their bodies. Their clothes were singed and torn, their faces weary, but they had come to see her anyway. Just as they had stayed to help instead of running, despite their fear of whatever was chasing them.

It was suddenly clear to Qi that all Lucky and Trick had were the clothes on their backs and each other.

And it's enough, Qi thought. *Love strong enough to survive an event like this is a magic more powerful than any Arcane or Divine.*

As Lucky sniffled and squeezed Trick's hand, a flicker of understanding ran through Qi. She'd been so focused on her study, she'd forgotten to consider the human element.

Trick and Lucky were looking for a way out of Altaea, just as she was looking for a way in. They needed a home, just as she did. And they were running now, just as her own grandparents had done all those years ago. It didn't matter where from, or even why. Only that they were desperate.

People didn't leave their homes unless there was nothing left for them there.

"I'm glad you are both all right," said Qi, eyes back on her work. "All of Midport might have been lost. A few notes needing to be re-written is a small price to pay."

Besides the house, of course, but Qi didn't say that. Her adventurers had suffered enough.

"Is there anything we can do?" Lucky asked, her eyes full of tears.

Qi paused. Was there?

She should despise them for destroying her home, her grandfather's door. But if they hadn't, she would have never discovered the apostate's secret. In a strange way, she was in their debt.

"Yes," Qi said. "There are two things."

"Name it," Lucky said quickly, but Qi turned her attention to Trick. The Arcane man seemed ready to resign himself to a tongue-lashing, but he eyed her steadily. He probably felt he deserved it. Qi understood the sentiment. Arcanes tended to internalise their shame to a greater degree than regular people.

"First, I need your honesty," said Qi. "Can you sense me?"

Trick frowned. They both knew what she meant.

There was a long, pointed silence, while Lucky's head bounced between the two of them hoping one would explain. The only sound came from the discordant tapping of her chipped fingernails on the wooden table. Qi remained unbothered, continuing to scribe the last of her notes on the events before their first meeting.

"No," Trick said carefully, the creases between his eyes deepening. "I cannot. A side effect of the fire?"

"You could say that," replied Qi.

A perfect half-truth.

She was getting rather good at them.

"What's the other thing?" asked Lucky, a little pouty at being left out of the conversation. She picked at the sides of her nails while her leg jittered under the table, some semblance of her regular self returning. "What can I do? I was going to try and fix your glasses, but you've done that already."

Qi finally paused in her writing. She carefully balanced her quill upon the ink pot, before disappearing under the table to rummage around in her satchel. She produced a large coin purse and tossed it onto the table in front of them. It thudded and clinked dramatically, drawing eyes from the nearest table, but Qi did not care.

"You can take the rest of your payment," she said.

Trick and Lucky both froze, their faces wearing twin expressions of astonishment.

"You cannot be serious," said Trick, spluttering. "We cannot accept it. We did not complete the job. The curse... My fire... I almost destroyed Midport. Seven realms, Qi, I burned down your house!"

"And then I dumped half of the Alsuran ocean on it!" added Lucky. She tried to push the coin purse towards Qi without upsetting any of the papers on the table.

"You're joking," she said, flailing her hands wildly in protest. "You have to be. Are you feeling well?"

"Never better," said Qi.

It was true. Despite the grievous loss, Qi finally had what she'd spent most of her life searching for. Her theories tested in the real world. Evidence that apostate could be bested. And a way to honour her family's legacy. The tempered apostate hanging around her neck was proof of that. No Arcane, not even the worst of the

Seven's sensors, could identify her as a magic user as long as she wore it. Even if nothing else came of it, she would use that advantage to claim her family home.

She could start again. Restore what she could. Rebuild. Honour her grandfather—both his Arcane ways and the everyday struggle to provide a better life for her family. The true soul of the home had been burned away long before a single flame ever touched it, and now it was Qi's turn to breathe life into it once more.

Qi glanced sideways—not at the stack of papers she had already completed, but the makeshift paperweight upon them. The piece of wood bearing the river lily carving did not move, glow, or hum; there was no reason to believe it held even a spark of the Arcane magic used to create it. But looking at it still brought her a sense of peace. It was almost like having her grandfather with her. In her heart, she knew he would approve of her decision.

"Please, take it," Qi said, waving at the coin purse with the end of her quill. "You've earned it, more than you know. Besides, if I remember correctly, you've got a ship to catch. I hear The Ruby Isles are beautiful this time of year."

They deserve their chance at freedom.

There was a tense silence, before Lucky launched herself across the table and pulled Qi into a tight embrace. Papers scattered, an ink pot went flying, and an ale mug teetered dangerously towards the edge before Trick caught it.

Qi bore the physical affection uncomfortably, blinking over Lucky's shoulder at Trick, who could only shrug and hide his soft chuckle behind his scarred hands. A single tear escaped his eye before he hurriedly brushed it away. Despite his anguish at causing the blaze, he looked less troubled than he had on their first meeting. Lighter. More hopeful.

Lucky squeezed so tight Qi was in danger of losing her ability to breathe. When she finally gave an odd squeak of protest, Lucky withdrew, but not before whispering in Qi's ear.

"You've saved our lives," said Lucky. "I'm going to name our first daughter after you."

Qi had no idea what to do with that information.

"Well," she said, readjusting her glasses and stacking her papers into an orderly pile once more. "Then I suppose they'll be the luckiest Qi in the Ruby Isles."

A FINAL NOTE FROM PROFESSOR YARRIX

The following is scribbled on the back of the last page of Qi's completed research paper in obnoxious shimmering emerald ink:

And there you have it, Eveka.

Although the apostate was not bested by magical means alone, it was eventually circumvented by utilising both Arcane and Divine Gifts driven by the most basic of human emotions.

As well as discovering the first known weakness in apostate's anti-magic properties, I believe Miss Picolas has also recorded an excellent example of how physical barriers such as the door can become our largest obstacle, far greater than any posed by magic. The mundane can no longer be overlooked.

Those like you and I have been using the Weave and the Gifts to attempt to locate the Architects for aeons—I propose we turn to more mundane methods. Perhaps we can even enlist our own

band of plucky unwitting adventurers to solve our problem for us.

After all, Kalar's very existence was seeded with shattered strands of the Weave and clueless infantile Gods, and still the people of this realm survived. Whether by mundane tricks or sheer luck, they fought for each other, and against all odds, they flourished.

It is enough to ponder whether the missing Architects are even necessary to repair what is broken in this universe. Perhaps the key to humanity's salvation is something more mundane: empathy.

All they need is a reason to open the door—or to burn it down altogether.

THE END

ACKNOWLEDGEMENTS

Firstly, as always, I would like to thank my family—my husband Matt, both for being the original Weaver of the Kalaraak story as it unfolded at the D&D table, and for supporting me through my writing journey. My children, Kira and Jensen, for leaving me alone for five minutes so I could actually get some words on the page, and also for being endless reminders to appreciate the beauty of silliness.

My editor and chief proof-reader, Kate Vandelay—I don't think I can express how invaluable your input is, and I'm forever grateful we have a decade of friendship forged by vodka raspberries at various pop punk nightclubs so I can claim first dibs on your services when you've blown up and are editing for authors much bigger than I am.

My writing group, the Break Ins—for offering support, beta reads, memes, and a guaranteed hype train whenever any one of us so much as mentions a book.

And double thank you for putting our secret project on the backburner, so *The Door* had a chance to shine on its own. Special thanks to Rob Leigh and Nicholas Fuller for beta-reading this story.

My cover artist, Mike Knot—it's uncanny how you can take a couple of shoddy sketches and a pinterest mood board and somehow create the exact image from my brain. Your art belongs in a museum.

My best friends Steph and Emily—y'all didn't have anything to do with *The Door* but I'm thanking you anyway. Ok love u bye.

The "Spark Fan Club", especially Esmay, Bob & Kylee—thank you for getting excited every time I show my face on the internet, and for continuing that excitement when you realised my next release wasn't *Spark of the Divine's* immediate successor. Your ARC reading, post sharing, and general hyping up are a big part of why I continue to do this.

And you, if you're reading this—people who read all the acknowledgements are extra special. Much of the world feels like an ongoing trash fire right now; I hope *The Door* offered you a few hours of escapism. May you always have the courage to kick down any doors blocking your own happiness.

If you enjoyed The Door, check out the first novel in the Kalaraak Chronicles:

HOW FAR WOULD YOU GO FOR YOUR GOD?

Mae wields her Divine gifts quietly, working as a mercenary—until a simple rescue job has her uncover a plot to steal power from the gods. When the god Mae serves is attacked, she must find a way to restore their divinity before the entire seven realms are thrown into chaos. But each member of Mae's crew has their own agenda, and forbidden romance and whispers of betrayal threaten to break them apart.

Spark of the Divine follows a group of reluctant heroes on a quest to save a god—as the fate of their realm hangs in the balance. Will they each find what they desperately seek, or will the secrets they keep from one another be their undoing? Can they master their fears to defeat an evil their world has never seen?

Is it the strength of the god that matters, or the belief of the Divine?

ABOUT THE AUTHOR

Louise Holland has been writing stories since around 1996, although her first official novel debuted in 2023. She lives in Adelaide, Australia, and spends her non-writing time with her family, her D&D party, or 1400 hours deep into Baldur's Gate 3.